Playing With Fire

Tiffany LaTanza

ISBN: 978-0-6151-5648-4

Victory by Design Press Publishing

Dallas

Published by Victory by Design Press

First Printing

ISBN: 978-0-6151-5648-4

Published by Victory by Design Press

www.victorybydesignpress.com

Printed in the United States of America

ACKNOWLEDGEMENTS

I thank God for blessing me with goals and ambition during a time when I felt like such a loser. I thank God for loving me just the way that I am and for giving me a voice. God is my everything and without him I am nothing. God, you are so…. "Ummph"…there are no words available to describe what you mean to me. There are no words that measure up. I thank you Father for being my deliverer, my healer, my way out of no way, my peace of mind, my redeemer, my protector….I'll be here all day if I say all that God is to me so I'll just say, Lord, you're my everything. I love you.

I would like to thank my earthly father, Bobby Daniels for always believing in me and encouraging me to be all that I can be. I pray that one day I can be just as successful as you. I love you.

I thank Pastor Curtis D. Lynch for loving me just like I'm one of his own. Although I'm not biologically yours, you still love me the same as all of your other kids. You have been so much more than a "step-father" to me which is why I rarely use the word "step-father" when I'm referring to you. I like to call you Dad #2. I love you.

To Tanza Lynch, words can't express how much I appreciate all the things that you've done for me. You are always there when I need someone to talk to or a shoulder to cry on. You're there to listen to all of my complaints about life and you're even there to put me in my place when I need it. I love you, Mommie and I couldn't have asked for a better mother. (Oh, and thanks for reading through all my books and catching my grammatical errors….LOL)

I'd also like to thank Tandi Fergerson for helping me edit my books and for all the promoting and marketing you've done for my books. You've played a very important part in my success and you've been with me every step of the way. Thanks.

Thank you, Clyde and Keoki Odems for investing in me and believing in my endeavors. You guys are family to me and I love you both. (and the kids)

Thank you Candace for my beautiful cover. You are truly awesome at what you do and are truly gifted. Keep up the good work.

And last but certainly not least, I'd like to thank my incredibly sexy husband, Steven T. Myers. What can I say? We've been together for eight years and I'm still just as in love with you as I was when I was sixteen. You're always there to catch all of my tears when I'm feeling discouraged or like I'm not going to make it. You're always there to comfort me when I'm feeling depressed. And you always know just the right things to say and the right things to do to always make me feel better about my situations. I couldn't have asked for a better husband and I thank God for making us for each other. I read my books to you over and over and over and over again and you never complain. You laugh as though I was reading it to you for the first time. I really appreciate you and I'll love you forever and be forever yours.

Oh, I almost forgot! Thank you to all of my fans. I appreciate you guys so much for all of your comments and positive criticism. I love you guys! I hope you enjoy Playing With Fire as much as you enjoyed Lord, Help Me. I pray that each book will be even better than the last.

Also, if you're an undiscovered author and would like to be published, please visit www.VictoryByDesignPress.com or send me an email at VictorybyDesignPress@Yahoo.com. Be sure and tell me what the book is about, if it has been copyrighted and a name, number and email address where you can be reached. God bless you.

"Quotes from the Mistress"

"This thing called love can really mess you up. Love can totally control your life and consume your soul without you even knowing it. Lust is the most famous seductress known to mankind. Some women may not ever understand how a woman could ever mess with another woman's man. Or in my case mess with her best friend's man. Honestly, I don't understand it either. How could a man make me betray the ones closest to me? I've hurt so many people with this affair, but what can I say? Love is an uncontrollable human emotion that can be spun out of control like a derailed rollercoaster. This man was not just any man. He was THE man. The man that made me feel like I was walking on air, the man that placed my every emotion into a pillar of excitement, the man that sexed me like no other man ever did before, not even my husband, the man that told me all the right things and touched me in all the right places, and the man whose kiss was like fire and ice that froze my body to it's core and burned me down to my soul. What was it about this man that drove me sexually insane? This man changed my life for the better and for the worst. Here's my story."

Prologue

"Whores, dogs and liars"

"Hey girl!" I said picking up the phone knowing exactly who was on the other end.

"Hey, Sash. Girl, I am so glad you're home." Requelle said in a tired shaky voice.

"Why? What's up?" I asked pretty sure of what the answer would be.

"It's Sylus. He didn't come home last night. Have you seen him?"

"Um….no I haven't. I'm sorry, girl." I said lying through my teeth.

"I don't understand him sometimes, Sash. He says he loves me and he can't live without me but he keeps doing shit like this! I don't understand why he keeps doing this to me." Rae cried.

"He keeps doing this to you because you keep letting him."

"I know but I can't help it. I love that man to death, Sash. What am I supposed to do?"

I was the last person she should have been asking that.

"Look Rae, I know you're hurting but I'm not the person you should be talking to about this. Wait for Sylus to come back and talk this thing out with him." I said exhaling a big sigh of guilt.

"I guess you're right. I'll talk to you later."

"I love you, girl."

"I love you too." She said hanging up the phone.

"Who was that on the phone, Baby?" Sylus asked coming out of the bathroom.

"It was your wife, Sy." I said rolling my eyes at him.

"What did she want?"

"Sy, you know what she wanted. Look, I can't do this anymore!" I said standing to my feet and throwing my hands in the air.

"What do you mean *you can't do this anymore?* Sasha…Baby, I love you." He said stepping closer to me and wrapping his strong arms around my waist.

"Requelle is my best friend and I'm tired of lying to her. I feel like such a whore, Sylus. This is wrong! I thought I could handle this but I can't!" I yelled pulling away from his grip.

"You're married to *my* best friend too! We've already done the deed and it ain't no turning back now. If I wasn't in love with you, I could just leave and go home to my wife never to see you again, but that's not the case. You mean the world to me, Sasha. I don't think I would be able to live without you." He said pulling me back into his broad chest and kissing me on the neck.

He knows that's my spot.

"Sylus, stop." I whispered.

"I can't." He whispered back.

"Sylus, you have to stop. Cornelius will be home from his business trip soon." I said feeling uneasy and turned on all at the same time.

"Say my name again." He seductively whispered.

"Sylus, I can't…."

Before I could even get my sentence out, Sylus had already ripped my Babyphat skirt and panties off and glided himself inside of me. My mind was telling me to stop but my body was saying otherwise. No one could ever make me feel as good as Sylus could. Not even my husband, Sylus' best friend, Cornelius. Don't get me wrong, Corn can put it down in the bedroom but Sylus had a way of making me feel like I was on top of the world and the universe was my sanctuary. I knew this was wrong but there was just something about Sylus that was so hypnotic. I could never say no to him no matter how hard I tried. I'm not sure if I truly love him or if I just love the way he makes love to me. I guess time will tell. Time never lies.

Chapter One

"Where it All Began"

Requelle and I have been best friends for almost eleven years. We've known each other since we were in the eleventh grade. We went to Connie C. Hart High. Requelle molded me into the person that I am today. She taught me how to love myself and how to defend myself.

I remember the very first time that I met her. It was back in 1994. I had just moved to Atlanta from Wylie, Texas. My parents had just gotten a divorce and my father left my mom and me to fend for ourselves. He wiped out all the bank accounts, packed his bags and left. I haven't seen my daddy since. I was all my mom had. We went from riches to rags in just 2 months. My mom still had the house but my dad failed to pay the bills leaving us broke, hungry…and two months later, *homeless*. So, my Aunt Lyla said we could come and stay with her for a few months until we got back on our feet. Aunt Lyla didn't exactly live in luxury. She stayed in the Lemon Tree projects located in the deep sticks on the west side of Atlanta. Well, a few months turned into a few years. My mom had a very hard time finding a job. She had been a housewife for over fifteen years. She didn't have any work experience. All she knew how to do was cook, clean and plant flowers. She never even finished high school because she got pregnant with me in the middle of her sophomore year in high school. I guess my mom just couldn't take it anymore. One Saturday morning I went to ask her what she wanted for breakfast and I found her with her face buried in the toilet and small white pills scattered all over the black tile floor. I ran over to her and flipped her body over and discovered two bloody razors embedded in the palms of her hands. The toilet was filled with blood and vomit. That was by far the worst day of my life. I felt so alone. Not only did my father throw me away but my mom has left me too. I was so angry at her. And unfortunately, the anger never went away.

My first day of school that year was horrible. It seemed as though everybody hated me before they even knew me.

"Look at Miss. *Thang*! She think she all dat just because she's from the big rich state of Texas! I bet they ride they big fancy horses to school over there. And look at her clothes. She dresses like a White girl!" They would say to me.

My mom and I may have been homeless and broke but we did manage to salvage the best of our expensive name brand clothes. The other kids were so jealous that I had such nice clothes but yet I stayed in the projects just like they did. They hated me because I had "good hair" and green eyes. They despised me because I spoke proper English and could afford braces on my teeth. All the other kids would tease me and say my braces looked like train tracks.

At lunch time that day, this stupid girl named Kasha, *who I still can't stand to this day,* tripped me with her foot as I was leaving the lunch line with my tray of meatloaf covered in tomato sauce and mashed potatoes. I had meat sauce all over my white Gucci shirt and miniskirt. I was furious.

"Oohh, my bad White girl! I didn't mean to trip you. Are you okay?" She asked sarcastically.

I said nothing. I began cleaning myself up with a balled up paper towel that I found on the shiny white cafeteria floor.

Kasha stepped in my face and pushed my shoulder with the tips of her ashy fingers.

"You ain't got nothin to say, rich girl?" She yelled me.

"No," I said in a quiet shy voice. I don't know why I let her treat me like that. It's not that I was afraid of her. I guess I just didn't want any trouble on my first day of school. And plus I've always been the type of person to just let stuff roll off my back. My Aunt always told me to just take it with a grain of salt and get over stuff.

"I know you hear me, *slut!* You are so stupid! I see why yo daddy left you, you ain't worth shit!" She yelled at me.

A crowd began to form a circle around us. *She just made this personal.* I stood there with my fist balled up and my jaw clenched tight.

"What? What you gone do, nigga?! You ain't gone do nothing because you know I'll whoop that tail!" She began walking away laughing.

"*She* may not do nothing, but I damn sho will!" A pretty girl with shiny shoulder length hair said stepping out into the middle of the circle and taking off her big gold hoop earrings. I had no idea who she was but she was by far one of the prettiest girls I had ever seen. She was chocolate skinned, had big brown eyes and she was very athletically built.

Kasha turned around. "Are you asking for a beat down, Requelle?" She asked with a devilish smile on her face.

"No, I think you're asking for one, *Trick!*" She said stepping in her face and pulling her hair up into a ponytail. Kasha balled up her fist and punched Requelle right in the nose. Blood immediately began to spill out. Requelle acted as though she didn't even feel it. She grabbed Kasha by her nappy hair and threw her to the ground. Kasha spit in her face. Requelle socked her right in the eye! I felt like I needed to do something even though Requelle was pretty much taking care of it. I jumped in and began pounding on Kasha with my fists. With each blow to Kasha's face, all I could think about was how mad I was. I thought about my father leaving me, I thought about how my mom had to prostitute herself just to pay the bills, I thought about how my whole family pretty much turned their backs on me. I had mentally gone to another place and when I finally came back to myself, Kasha was covered in blood, sweat, tears and saliva. My hands hurt so bad. The skin around my knuckles was completely gone. Requelle and I beat the hell out of that girl. We almost killed her. She was in the hospital for three weeks. Requelle and I were suspended for two weeks and luckily no charges were pressed. From that point on, we had become the very best of friends.

Chapter Two

"It's your play"

This weekend marks the eleventh year anniversary of my friendship with Requelle. We always take a trip on anniversary weekend. This year we're going to Orlando, Florida. Our husbands are coming along too.

"I wish they would hurry up and get here," I said to my husband, Cornelius.

"Babe, they said they were on their way. Just be patient. They'll be here in a minute," He said getting annoyed.

"Oh, there they are! Requelle! Requelle!" I yelled as I jumped up and down like a child suffering from ADHD.

"Sashaaaaaa!" She yelled back being just as goofy.

"Girl, traffic was a beast this evening. I had like five road rage episodes trying to get here! Hey, Corn. How are you?" She said giving Cornelius a hug.

"I'm good, Rea. How are you?" He responded giving her a kiss on the cheek.

"Oh, I'm great!"

"What's up, Sylus? I haven't seen you on the court lately. Scared?" Corn said with a smirk.

"Man, whatever! Nigga, you act like you got some game or something! Ain't nobody scared of your no ball playin behind." Sylus laughed giving him a one armed hug.

We all talked and laughed for another ten minutes and then finally boarded the plane. We were in first class like movie stars. Sylus is a friend of the pilot so he hooked us up. Sylus has a lot of hook ups. He's our local everything. He's an extremely gifted singer and can play six different instruments; piano, drums, guitar, saxophone, harp and the violin. He's best at the sax. Sylus is a genius. He excels in almost everything that he attempts. He's very intelligent. Sylus has a B.S. in biochemistry and music education. He was accepted into med-school immediately following college and is now a very successful pediatrician. He and Requelle have been together since high school. I remember when they first met.

Homecoming Dance

1995

Tomorrow is the homecoming dance. Requelle was nominated homecoming queen for the third year in a row. Requelle has always been "Miss. Popularity". She's on the volleyball team, the track team, the chess team, the step team, she's in the drama club, and she's class secretary. And on top of all that, she's a straight A student. She's in the top 2% of our class. Requelle could definitely go far in life if she would just handle up on her little anger problem. She will fight at the drop of a hat. She ain't scared of nobody and never will be. She's been that way since the very first day that I met her.

"Sasha, you still haven't picked out your dress? Girl, the dance is tomorrow! What is wrong with you," Requelle yelled at me.

"Look, I don't have money to buy a dress right now." I said playing with my pink press on nails.

"All those expensive clothes you got and you ain't got not one formal gown?"

"No, all I have are casual clothes. I would have just bought me one but I had to pay my aunt's rent and you know Rusty's Burger Barn ain't exactly a *good* paying job. You know she's sick and can't work right now," I sighed.

My Aunt Lyla was diagnosed with breast cancer about six months ago. She said the doctors say she has less than two years to live. She's not taking it well at all. Aunt Lyla won't eat, shower or speak to anyone, not even me. She makes it seem like it's my fault she has cancer. All she does is yell and scream at me all the time.

"Okay, I know a way we can get you a dress. Do you trust me?" She asked with a look of deceit in her eyes.

"Yeah…Rae, what are you thinking up?"

"Come on let's go!" She said yanking me off the care bear printed twin size bed.

Roaches scattered as we ran through the dark two bedroom project apartment and flew out the front door.

Requelle drove us in her mom's 1993 Altima to a boutique called Princess Shop. It was one of those ritzy shops. Just a pair of socks will run you about fifty dollars. There was a dress in the window that would look perfect on me. It was a light peach two piece with white pinstripes. It had a v shaped top that ran almost to the middle of the stomach area that tied around the neck and the back was totally exposed. The skirt was long and had about a one foot train. It was beautiful.

"Rea, what are we doing here? We can't afford anything in here." I said as I pulled her by the neck collar.

"Trust me, okay? That dress in the window would look great on you. I can almost picture it on you." She said taking an imaginary picture of me.

We walked in and the snobby sales ladies stared at us. As we began walking around I noticed that we were being followed like a pair of criminals.

"Excuse me; can I help you find something?" The lady asked turning her nose up at me.

"No, we're just looking. Is that okay with you?" I asked sarcastically.

"Yes, that's fine with me. Just make sure you *look* and don't *touch*. I don't need you putting your little nasty hands all over things that you know you can't afford."

My jaw almost fell to the floor. I couldn't believe she was treating me like that! How did she know we didn't have any money? I rolled my eyes at her, snatched the dress off the dummy in the window, grabbed Requelle and went into the dressing room.

"Sash! That dress is beautiful! You have to get it!" I looked down at the price tag and almost fainted.

"Rae, this dress is *twenty five hundred dollars*! How will I ever be able to afford this?" I said quickly taking the silky dress off and putting it back on the hanger.

"Don't worry. I know where a secret door is." She smiled at me. I had no idea what she was talking about but I went with it anyway. I stuffed the dress into my purple Nike backpack and put my clothes back on.

"Follow me." She said

I followed her into a small hole that was located under the rug in the dressing room. It was a small cave like space that led us down into a tunnel. We finally crawled through a small opening at the end of the tunnel and ended up outside right in front of the car. We immediately hopped in and drove off. It seems that the boutique was having some foundation problems and the building was practically splitting in half.

The whole ride home was very stressful for me. I've always had a guilty conscience. Even though those sales people treated us badly, we still had no right to go in and take something that didn't belong to us. My mom always told me, "You're not held accountable for what other folks do to you but you are held accountable for what you do to other folks." Requelle didn't seem bothered by our actions at all. But I was bothered. I guess we were exactly what the sales ladies thought we were...*thieves.*

Once I got home I immediately dropped to the floor. I was so stressed out about what happened that I stressed myself right to sleep. I could feel the roaches crawling over my toes and fingers. I finally woke up when I felt one crawling in my ear. "I hate these damn roaches!" I yelled brushing them off. I looked at the apple clock on the dirty kitchen wall and realized it was almost an hour before the dance. I had thirty minutes to get ready. Once I got my dress on, I felt like an African princess. As the door bell rang, I snatched my handbag off the cluttered wooden countertop and ran for the front door.

"Ooohhh, girl! You look *damn* good in that dress! I am so lucky to have you as my date tonight." Cornelius said opening the car door for me. Cornelius is this smooth talking light skinned brotha that I met several months ago. We've actually been in school together since freshmen year but I didn't officially meet him until just recently. He's pretty nice but he's a thug. He's a part of this gang called PAP's which stands for "Pretty Ass Pimps". I like to pretend that I don't know. That way my conscience can't bother me. He had on a peach suit and peach alligator shoes that matched my dress to the T. Cornelius was sharp!

We walked into the dance and immediately ran for the dance floor. Cornelius was not a *bad* dancer but he wasn't a good one either.

"So...Are you having a good time?" He asked.

"Yeah...are you?"

"Oh, yeah! I love spending time with you. I know I just met you a few months ago and everything...and you really don't know me...but do you see this going anywhere or was I just your date for tonight?" He asked grabbing my hands.

"Um...I don't know. I mean...I really like you, if that's what you're asking. I wouldn't mind us going out again." I smiled at him.

"Cool." He responded.

"Hey will you come with me to look for my friend? Or you can stay here and dance if you want. I won't get jealous." I said giggling.

"If you promise me that you'll come back, I'll stay here and wait for you." He said giving me a soft kiss on the lips.

A big smile formed on my face. "Okay, I'll be right back."

I looked for Requelle for over an hour. I looked all over the dance floor and she was nowhere to be found. I finally began looking around the dark empty halls of the school. I heard mumbling coming from inside one of the lonely classrooms. I cut the corner and found Requelle kneeled down on her knees with some chocolate brotha's *ding-a-ling* in her mouth. I ain't never even seen this dude before. I didn't know what to do so I just stood there staring. With each pulse I grew more and more angry. Unfortunately, this was not the first time that I've seen this in my lifetime. Watching my best friend do that made me remember how many times I had to watch my mom do that. My mom would have sex while I was right in the same room sometimes. She would just tell me to look the other way. Some days, she would be doing more than one man at a time.

"There you are. Are you okay, Baby?" Cornelius asked walking around the corner.

Requelle heard him and stopped what she was doing mid pulse. The chocolate brotha began putting himself back into his pants and cheesing like something was funny. Cornelius walked up and was as shocked as I was.

"Sash, how long were you standing there?" Requelle asked with worry in her voice.

"I…I'm sorry. I didn't mean to interrupt. Um…Rae, what are you doing? Who is this guy and why were you doing that with him? Never mind…I'm sorry. I'll see you at school on Monday. Bye." I said grabbing Cornelius and walking away. Rae ran and caught up with me.

"Sash, don't be like that. I was just having fun with him, ok?" She said with a smile on her face.

"I watched my mom do that to a different man every hour and it didn't look like fun to *me!*" I screamed.

"Sasha, calm down. It is not a big deal." Cornelius said grabbing my hand. Requelle knew how sensitive I was about sex. She knew and understood why I was being so dramatic.

"What I do has absolutely nothing to do with you. I'm sorry your mom was a whore, Sash. She did what she had to do to take care of you. I'm just having fun. By the way, this is Sylus." She said pointing over at him.

"I'm sorry we had to meet under these circumstances…but it's nice to meet you, Sasha. My mom was a prostitute too so I know exactly how you feel. I'm sorry you had to see that. I hope you accept my deepest apology." He said reaching out his hand.

After looking him up and down a few more times, I finally shook his hand. "This is Cornelius, my date. And I'm sorry I overreacted." Cornelius shook Sylus' hand and we all just stood there and eventually started laughing. Sylus was not even Requelle's date. She said the guy she came with was too boring so she had to kick him to the curb. She found Sylus walking outside on his way to the bus stop and scooped him up. *What a slut!* But that's my girl and I love her to death. We went back into the dance and had a good time. That was probably the best dance of the year. Requelle won homecoming queen.

We arrived at our hotel about three hours later. It was really nice. We were staying at the Paradise Hotel right off the highway next to the zoo. It was a big, white ten story building surrounded by tropical flowers of all colors. It was very pretty. We walked in and was so amazed at how beautifully decorated the lobby was. It literally looked like an indoor tropical paradise. It had dark wooden floors, bright red, blue and orange chairs and sofas, beautiful floral decorations and big white marble desks.

"Hi, we're here to check in." Sylus said reaching for his wallet.

"Okay, Sir. Can I see your ID and credit card please?" The Indian lady requested. Sy pulled them out and showed them to her.

"Okay. You two will be in room 507 and the other two will be in 714."

"Excuse me but these rooms were supposed to be together. Can you make this happen please?" Sy said in a stern voice.

"I'm so sorry Sir. But all of our rooms are booked. These are the last two available." She said sincerely.

We all agreed to the rooms that were offered and proceeded to locate them. Cornelius and I were in room 507. We were in the African culture suite. Each room had a different theme. The room was very cultured but it made me a little uncomfortable. I did the best I could to ignore all the slave statues they had sitting around. I eventually couldn't take it anymore and threw them all in the closet.

"This is nice, huh Baby?" Corn said plopping himself unto the bed.

"Yeah, this is nice. We got a big screen TV, a DVD player, a Jacuzzi tub, a full size sofa and a king size bed. This is great!" I said trying to figure out which remote went to the TV.

"King size bed, huh? Let's go try it out." He said with this stupid smile on his face.

"We can't. Rae and Sy are coming to our room to play uno until the movie starts." I said running around the couch trying to get away from him. We were going to see the second installment of Harry Potter. Of course, the men picked that one.

"Come on, Sasha." He whined.

"No. The second we get undressed, you know they are going to knock on that door!"

"Fine, be that way!" He said throwing his hands up. He slowly eased up behind me and wrapped his muscular arms around me.

"What did I just say?" I asked batting my eyes.

"You know you can't resist all of this." He whispered in my ear. He stuck his tongue in my ear and began placing slow soft kisses on the back of my neck. *He knows that's my spot!*

"Oohh...you're not playing fair!" I said leaning my head back on his shoulder and closing my eyes. I turned around and melted into his mouth. He felt and tasted so good.

I've always felt blessed to have such a good marriage. Our marriage is nothing less than perfect. We make love every night sometimes more than once, we read to each other, we laugh and play with each other, we respect one another, we're honest with each other, we're faithful to each other, we care about each other and most of all we love each other. I couldn't have asked for a better man. It doesn't hurt that he's so incredibly sexy either. He has a perfectly ripped six foot six inch manila skinned body. He's ripped from head to toe. He has black curly hair. He wears it short, waved at the top and faded on the sides. He has dark brown eyes and the sexiest soft pink lips. I must admit that this man still knocks me off my feet.

Right as Corn began unbuttoning my pinstripe slacks, we were startled by a loud knock at the door.

"See, Corn! I told you they would interrupt us!" I screeched frantically looking for my black silk blouse.

"Okay, okay! I'll get the door." Corn came up behind me and whispered in my ear, "We'll finish this later."

"I'll think about it." I smiled.

Cornelius ran almost tripping over my high heel shoes trying to answer the door. I giggled at that.

"Who dat is?" He yelled being stupid.

"Um...this is Sister Mary Clark from down the way. Do you know Jesus young man? Do you have some Jesus in your life?" Sylus said in an old lady voice pretending to be a Jehovah's Witness. They both laughed and Corn finally opened the door. They gave each other a high five and a snap.

"Hey man. We didn't take too long did we? What were y'all up in here doing anyway?" Sy asked looking around.

"Non ya business Negro! You ready to get whooped in some uno?" Corn said throwing the deck of uno cards on the table.

"Man, please! Bring it on!" Sy laughed.

"You wanna put your money where your mouth is, my brotha?"

"A hundred dollars a game sound good?" Sy asked with confidence.

Corn responded, "Oh we have ourselves a game."

Once I got myself together, I walked out into the living area and sat down at the table.

"Oh, I know what y'all was doing!" Requelle said laughing and pointing at my zipper. I looked down and saw that it was wide open. My pooh bear panties were totally exposed. I was so embarrassed.

"Shut up and let's get this game started!" I snickered.

"So Sash, how are things going in the exciting world of forensics? I was really surprised that you quit nursing. You were an excellent nurse." Sy said.

"Um…you see a lot of strange and sad things working in my field. I loved it when I first started doing it a year ago but like everything else…it gets old. I don't think I can stomach it anymore." I said staring him in the face.

I began to notice how beautiful Sylus' light brown eyes were as I stared at him from across the table. He also has the most beautiful smile I had ever seen. During this very moment he'd never looked sexier. He's chocolate skinned and has beautiful full lips and a sexy goat tee. He wears his hair very low almost bald and wavy and he's the best dresser I know. He's not the normal type to catch my eye though. I like light skinned, pretty haired, tall muscular men. Sylus is none of the above. He's not exactly muscular but he's not fat or built wrong by any means. His body is definitely more than average. He's not exactly short but yet he's not tall either. He's about five foot nine or ten. He's just a victim of being caught right in between being fine and just okay if you go by looks alone. But Sylus definitely has a unique sexiness about him. Women have been captivated by him for as long as I've known him. Unfortunately, this is not the first time that I've been amused by his fineness. Back in college, I thought I was in love with Sylus.

Biology Class

2000

"Okay class! Settle down!" Mr. Heatherfield yelled trying to get us to be quiet.

The class settled down and began taking out notes to get ready for the review for the next exam that was coming up in three days. I hadn't even studied yet.

"Hey Sash! Have you studied for the exam this Friday?" Sylus asked jumping into his seat.

"Nope. Have you?" I asked picking a pin up off the floor.

"Nope. I haven't either. You want to study together? I figured we could help each other since our GPA's depend on this exam."

"Okay, that's cool. I'll meet you after school…say…around 5 or so?" I said raising my eyebrow.

"Okay, I'll catch up with you then."

We met at my apartment. Rae had to work until around 10 o'clock that night so we had the place to ourselves with no distractions. We began studying and Sylus was already distracted by a fly on the wall.

"Sy, are you listening to me? Pay attention or we are going to fail this exam and lose our scholarships!" I said throwing a text book at him.

"Hey! Why you playin'? I'm listening to you, girl!" He laughed throwing the book back and hitting me upside my head.

"Oh, no you didn't! It's on now!" I playfully jumped in his lap and wrapped my hands around his neck. We fell off the couch and landed on the floor. I fell on top of him and in the midst of my laughter he planted a soft kiss on my lips. I immediately got up off the floor and stood to my feet.

"Sy, what was that? Rae is my best friend and she loves you to death. I *won't* do this."

"Sash, I didn't mean for that to happen. I'm sorry, Baby I just got caught up in the moment. Please forgive me." He said picking himself up off the floor and straightening out the wrinkles in his shirt with the palms of his hands. Sy looked at me for a long second, pulled me closer to him and kissed me again. Only this one was on purpose and much deeper. And it felt damn good. I managed to pull myself away.

"I can't, Sy."

"Are you telling me that you didn't feel anything? I can't help it, Sash, I'm sorry. You do something to me. I've been able to restrain myself for this long but I'm about to burst. You make me break all my rules. You make me crazy. I want you…" He said plopping back down on the couch and burying his face in his hands.

"Sy…I don't know what to say. Of course I felt something but I wasn't supposed to. I…I don't know what you do to me either. One minute I hate you and the next…I can't stop thinking about you. I want you too. In fact, I think I might love you." I said sitting down next to him and letting out a big sigh. I couldn't believe that I had just said that.

"I love you too." He responded.

I never told Rae or Corn about that day or any of the other times we kissed. We carried on a secret relationship for probably about a year or so but eventually the flame blew out and Sy and I realized that what we felt wasn't love. It was an infatuation or lust even. Plus, we were tired of the drastic measures we had to take to see each other. We agreed to take that secret to the grave with us and never speak a word of it again. Sometimes it kills me knowing that I've betrayed the two people that I love the most. But other times I figure…*what they don't know won't hurt them.*

"Well if you get out of the field you're in now, what field are you thinking about going into? I always thought you would pursue your cooking skills. You're the best cook I know. You're going to have to come over and teach me how to make your famous chicken alfredo." He said licking his lips. His lips looked so sweet and juicy.

"Yeah, I'll do that, Sy." I said laughing.

Sylus' hypnotic stares haunted me from across the table throughout the uno game. I thought maybe I had a booger in my nose or something but that wasn't it. Sylus and I caught eye contact about once every two minutes. I felt like he was trying to tell me something with his eyes. *Man he has some pretty eyes. And those lips…I just want to kiss them to see if they're as soft as they were in college.*

"Sash!" Requelle yelled.

I wiped the imaginary drool off my bottom lip. "Huh…what…I mean…"

Rae laughed, "Were you having a moment or something? It's your play, silly!"

"Oh, my bad." I said smiling and looking down at my cards.

As I played my hand I felt a gentle push on my foot under the table. I thought it was Corn playing footzies. But it was Sylus. He rubbed the bottom of my foot with his and stared directly into my eyes for at least five minutes. I was surprised that neither Rae nor Corn noticed. I didn't know what to think or say. I just stared back at him as he stared at me. I didn't quite understand why I was all of a sudden so fascinated with him again. He just looked so damn good in that light blue silky collar shirt. Sylus finally mouthed the words, "We need to talk." And from that moment on I knew that we had just started something and nothing would be the same from that point on.

Chapter Three

"Dejavu"

I just can't get Sylus out of my head. I tried to pretend that I wasn't attracted to him and that I didn't want him but it's getting harder and harder as the days go by. Maybe once we get off this vacation I can go back to being my normal self. Maybe that's what it is. Once we get back home, I'm almost sure this will go away.

"Hey you." Sy said walking up behind me.

"Hey. What are you doing out here? I thought you were afraid of water." I said laughing and splashing water on him from the sparkling blue pool.

"Ha Ha, very funny." He said sarcastically.

"No, really…what are doing out here?"

"I actually saw you out here from the hotel window so I came down. Rae is sleep so I was kind of bored. Where's Corn?" He asked raising his pant legs and sticking his feet in the pool.

"Oh, he went to the gym to workout. Sy…the other night you said we needed to talk. What's up?"

"I…I mean…never mind. I don't want to cross any lines here." He said staring at me.

"No, just tell me. This is between me and you." I said pulling myself out of the pool and sitting on the edge next to him.

"Okay, Sash…I could be wrong but has something happened between us?"

"What do you mean?" I asked knowing exactly what he meant.

"I think you know what I mean, Sash. Are you kind of feeling me again?" He said scooting closer to me.

"Um…I don't know. I guess…well…are you?"

"Yes, very much so. I can't get you out of my mind. I can't stop thinking about you, dreaming about you, talking about you…I don't know what's happening between us. But I do know that I want you and I don't know why." He belched out taking a deep breath.

"Sy, I thought what we had was over. What are we doing? Why put ourselves through this again?"

He scooted closer to me and gripped my chin with the tip of his thumb and his pointer finger. "I don't know, maybe because the feelings we once felt for each other are still just as strong. Maybe the only reason we stopped kicking it back in the day was because we felt guilty. Look, I'm not trying to come between you and Corn. I know that you two are happy. I don't want to love you but I do. I can't help it. I think we need to just deal with it."

"And how do you suppose we do that, Sy?" I said looking at him crazy.

"I don't have all the answers. Eventually, Corn and Rae are going to start noticing things between us. I try so hard not to treat you any differently but I can't help it."

"Look, I'm going to just leave this alone because I really don't want to go here again, ok?" I said picking myself up, grabbing my towel and walking away.

Sy ran up and grabbed me from behind. He whispered in my ear. "I'm sorry. I didn't mean to upset you. I just wanted you to know how I felt. The last thing I want to do is mess things up for you or hurt you. You can't honestly tell me that you don't love me, can you?" He asked moving his hand up the middle of my stomach and up to my breast.

"Sy, you know I love you. But can it be just that? Why make it into something that it doesn't have to be?" I asked getting annoyed and removing his hand from my breast.

He whipped me around to face him and gave me a slow peck on the lips. "No, it can't be *just that.*" His lips sent nervous chills up my spine.

"Sylus, what are you doing out here?" Rae yelled from across the other side of the pool.

I could literally see Sylus' heart about to jump out of his chest. He turned to me and stared at me like he had just seen a ghost.

"I was getting ice and saw you by the pool." He said so quickly that I could barely understand him.

"Hey, Baby! I was just getting some ice and I saw Sash by the pool." He yelled back across the pool.

"Oh, Sash, is that you?" Rae said with a smile on her face as she began walking over towards us.

"Oh, hey girl!" I said coming out from behind Sylus and waving my hand.

"I thought you were sleep." Sy said giving her a kiss on the cheek.

"I was but I noticed you weren't lying beside me so I came to look for you." She said with an unusual smile on her face.

She knows something.

"Well, I'm going to go and get cleaned up. I'll see you guys later on tonight." I said waving goodbye and walking away.

I knew by the panic in my stomach that this was going to turn out bad. I knew that Rae had to see something she just didn't know *WHAT* she saw. This should have been a clear sign that what Sylus and I were doing was going to lead to destruction. But sometimes when you let your emotions dictate your actions you don't pay attention to the signs. And that had to be one of the biggest mistakes of my life.

Chapter Four

"To Hell and back again"

Today marks day three. I still have four more days to go dealing with Sylus. I can't even function right. I can't sleep. I can't eat or even think. I can't help but wonder how this all came about. I told myself that I would never betray Cornelius like this again. I've never slept with Sy nor do I plan to but it's becoming harder and harder to sustain. I want to do right, *I really do* but I feel like my emotions are taking over like a state of hypnosis. I don't know what to do.

"Ahhh, it feels so good to lie down." Corn said slowly placing himself under the soft flower printed down covers. We had just spent the whole day at Six Flags. We were beat. Fortunately, I didn't have to deal with any drama with Sy today. He barely even spoke two words to me.

"Hey, did it seem like Sy was acting a little funny today?" Corn asked.

"Um…no, I didn't notice anything." I quickly responded.

"Are you sure? Because to me, he seemed a little distant like he had a lot on his mind or something. He was barely talking today. He just wasn't himself. You think we're smothering them or something? You think he maybe wants to spend some time with just him and Rae?" He said sitting up on the bed.

"Maybe." I responded.

I know Corn could tell that *I too* was acting a little suspiciously. But he's always been the type to just sit back and collect evidence and wait for me to screw up. Corn rolled over and fell asleep.

The next day, Corn and I decided to do something with just the two of us so that we could give Sy and Rae their space since it was obvious that they were having some issues. We were on our way to Chili's to eat. That's my absolute favorite restaurant. I order the same thing every time we go, *The Triple play*. My cell phone began to ring.

"Hello." I answered.

"Hey girl." Rae sighed. There was obviously something wrong.

"Hey. What's up? You and Sy were acting a little funny yesterday."

"Sash, its Sy. I think he's cheating on me again."

I almost choked on my gum. "What...I mean...why do you say that?"

"The last time he cheated on me, he just shut down. He wouldn't talk to me, we didn't make love, and he acted like he didn't even want to be around me. And now I'm getting that same feeling." She said sounding as though she was about to cry.

"Rae, maybe he's just tired or maybe he just needs some space. You know men have their *time of the month* too." I said hoping she would agree with me.

"No, Sasha. I know my husband. I thought all this cheating stuff was over but apparently it's not. I don't know why I even continue to stay with him. I don't have any ties to him. We don't have any kids or anything. I could just be out if I wanted to but something keeps making me stay. I don't understand why he keeps doing this to me. I don't deserve this. I've been faithful to him since day ONE! I just don't understand. You think it's something I'm doing wrong?" She began to cry.

"Rae, don't cry. Please don't. You're going to make me cry. No, don't blame yourself for something somebody else is doing. This is not your fault at all. I'm so sorry, Rae." I said as a tear ran down my face.

"You have nothing to be sorry about. *You're* not the one who's cheating, *he is!*" She responded. I felt so bad because technically, *I had cheated too.*

"Look, I don't mean to ruin you guys' evening with my problems. I'll put myself together and see you guys tomorrow. I love you, Sash."

"I love you too, Rae." I said hanging up the phone.

I had a stomach full of guilt. Everything in me was telling me to just spill the beans and deal with whatever consequences. But I knew that I couldn't...*not now.*

We arrived at Chili's three o'clock on the dot. We grabbed a corner booth right by the window. There was a beautiful pine tree standing right outside the window. It was such a beautiful tree so full of life and so free. "I wish I could be free." I whispered to myself. As I gazed out the window, I began reminiscing about my days as a young child. Back when everything seemed to be perfect. Back when my mom and dad were still together. I was so happy then. I remember our very last Christmas together. My daddy took us to Chili's because my mom was a terrible cook. I loved my father to death back then. I thought he could do no wrong until that day.

Christmas Day

1985

"Daddy, I want chicken crispers!" I yelled across the table jumping up and down on the booth bench.

"Okay, okay. Chicken crispers it is." He said tickling my stomach. I could get away with murder with my daddy. My daddy was a very successful man. He was an architect. I don't know exactly how much money he made a year but I knew it was a lot. It was enough to afford a five hundred thousand dollar home, two BMWs and a Lexus. He bought me whatever I wanted and then some. I always thought that my mom was jealous of the bond between my father and me. But that wasn't it at all.

"Honey, I'll have the chicken fried steak and mashed potatoes." Mom said closing her menu and setting it in the middle of the wooden table.

"I think not." Daddy said in a stern voice and jerking his head up. Mom seemed very startled by that.

"What are you talking about?" She asked.

"I don't mean to be mean but you've gained quite a bit of weight since having Sasha. I want you to go on a diet and lose some of the fat. You'll be having salad. I refuse to be seen with an disgusting fat woman. I'm too good for that." He said throwing the menu in her face. I didn't know what he was talking about. Mom looked great to me. She only weighed maybe one hundred and fifty pounds and she was the most beautiful woman I had ever seen.

"Kyle, don't do this. I'm tired of you trying to make me feel bad because I've gained fifteen pounds of weight!" Mom yelled.

Daddy slammed his heavy hand on the wooden table startling the poor waitress who had just walked up. Daddy didn't say a word. He just stared at Mom like she was crazy.

I felt like I needed to do something so I began ordering my food.

"I'll have chicken crispers and a chocolate milk." I said trying to hold back the tears.

"Okay, and you ma'am?" The waitress asked mom.

Mom looked Daddy right in the eyes, "I'll have the chicken fried steak and mashed potatoes."

Daddy immediately jumped across the table, grabbed Mom by the neck and pulled her out of the booth. The waitress ran to the bar and picked up the phone to call the police.

"DyAnn, what the fuck did I just tell you! Huh? You're not only fat and ugly but you're stupid too! Sasha, let's go!" He yelled back at me. I took a second look at the frantic waitress who was now in tears, and pulled myself out of the booth. I was so scared. I thought Daddy was going to kill us.

Once we got in the car, things went from bad to worse. Daddy couldn't even drive right because he was too busy beating Mom in the face and chest. He struck her over and over and over again until I just couldn't take it anymore.

"Daddy, stop! I hate you!" I screamed and began covering my ears.

He brought the car to a halt in the middle of the freeway and turned around and looked at me. "What did you just say to me little girl?" He said with his jaw clenched tight.

"I said I hate you!" I screamed again.

"Oh, do you?" He asked with a smirk on his face. At that moment I knew that *he* wasn't the daddy that I thought he was.

"Kyle, please. She didn't mean it. Don't hurt my baby, Kyle!" Mom managed to say going in and out of consciousness. He ignored her. Daddy turned around in his seat, unlocked the back door and swung it open. He pulled me by my long curly pony tail and chunked me out of the car onto the wet cold pavement. I was run over by two cars. Daddy then threw mom out of the car and drove off. We never saw him again.

Angels must have been watching over us that day. Some guy that we didn't even know stopped, picked us up and drove us to a hospital. Mom was okay. She had a fractured cheek bone and a lot of bruising. I on the other hand needed one hundred and fourteen stitches. I also had two broken ribs, a broken ankle and a broken finger. I don't know who that mystery man was that picked us up but I'm so thankful that he helped us out. Otherwise we may have died out there. He paid all of our medical bills and left us a black leather study Bible.

From that point on it was just me and my mom in a cold dark cruel world. The world that I knew was destroyed from that day forth.

"Sash? What's wrong, Baby?" Corn asked wiping a tear from my cheek.

"Nothing. I'm fine."

"Sasha, talk to me." He said turning my face towards his.

I finally responded. "I just don't understand why some people have it so good and yet people like me have it so bad. What did I ever do to deserve what I got? I've been drug through the pits of hell over and over again since I was 6 years old. I just don't understand why God is doing this to me but yet he wants me to give him all of the praise and all the glory. I think not! He doesn't deserve it!" I yelled slamming my fists on the table. I began to cry uncontrollably.

"Baby, you can't blame God for the cards that you were dealt. Our God is a loving God. There is a reason for everything, Sash. Weeping may endure for a night but joy cometh in the morning. What has happened that's causing all of these emotions to come out?" He asked holding me close.

"No, nothing's happened. I mean, I'm okay physically but mentally I'm torn up inside. Some mornings I wake up and pray that I can go back to sleep and never wake back up again. Honestly, you're the only reason I'm still here. If I didn't have you I would have killed myself a long time ago. I love you so much, Cornelius." I whimpered leaning my head on his shoulder.

"Don't talk like that." He said holding me close.

"I love you, Corn."

He smiled at me. "I love you too."

Chapter Five

"You've made your bed..."

Sy has been really working my nerves since the uno game. He always knows exactly what to say. He knows exactly where and what to touch and exactly what buttons to push to get an arousal out of me. I don't know how he does that to me. No matter how much I want to resist him, for some reason I just can't. His lips are so soft, his eyes are so hypnotic and his touch is so enchanting. How does a girl resist all of that?

"Hey You." Sylus said walking up behind me while I was in the bathroom getting ready to take a shower.

"Sy, I'm about to take a shower! How did you get in here? Where's Cornelius?" I said looking back at him in the crystal clear mirror.

Sy grabbed me by the waist, hugged me close and gave me a kiss on my boney shoulder. "Cornelius is gone. He went to the basketball court." He smiled.

"But what are you doing here?" I asked lifting my right eye brow.

"You know what I'm doing here." He said in a sexy voice. Sylus grabbed my face and planted a kiss on me that felt like no other. I almost melted. It was by far the best kiss I had ever tasted. It left a sensation so intense that I couldn't pull away. He ran his fingers from my face down to my neck, then to my belly button until he finally arrived between my legs. Sy then pulled my powder pink cotton robe off my caramel skinned naked body. He rubbed my body in all the right places. He smelled so good and felt even better. He slowly took off his shirt and unzipped his tan kaki pants. His chocolate body was so beautiful. Sy picked me up and pressed my body up against the blue tile shower wall with his. He slowly and gently slid himself inside of me. Sylus had a unique penetration that sent every part of me into ecstasy. Each stroke felt better and better. My silent whimpers became moans and my moans became screams.

"Sash! What are you doing?" Corn giggled loudly.

I awoke from my fantasy. "Huh? What?"

Corn walked closer to me with a curious frown on his face. "What were you doing?" He asked.

I swallowed hard. "Um…nothing. I mean…I was just daydreaming. Why? What are *you* doing?" I said trying to avoid the issue at hand.

"What do you mean what am *I doing*? I'm not the one sitting in an empty bathtub feeling myself up! Now, are you going to tell me what you were doing in here or do you want me to take a guess?" He said folding his muscular arms across his chest.

"I told you. I was just daydreaming. Please leave me alone Corn!" I said pushing him out of the bathroom and slamming the door.

I was so embarrassed. I don't even know how I dozed off like that. I mean I was awake but then I wasn't awake. I can only imagine how I looked laying butt naked in an empty bathtub with my hand buried between my legs. I must have looked like a horny fool!

I finally managed to collect myself and pull myself out of the bathroom after about two hours. Corn was sitting on the bed with a very concerned look on his face. I just kind of walked passed him not even acknowledging that he was there. Corn grabbed my hand covered in perspiration and sat me down on the bed next to him.

"What's going on, Sash? Are you not attracted to me anymore? Do I not satisfy you anymore?" He asked staring at me.

"Corn, no. You give me everything that I want and need." I said staring back at him.

"Then what's the problem? Why do you feel a need to make love to yourself when I'm standing right in the next room? I don't understand that! You know I'm always willing and ready to please you." He yelled.

"Look, I don't want to talk about this, okay? It's over!" I yelled back getting up off the bed.

He responded. "Yeah, you're right! This conversation is over! I'll meet you down stairs. We're meeting Sy and 'nem in fifteen minutes." Cornelius grabbed his wallet and stormed out the door letting it slam behind him.

Drama.

When I finally walked down stairs, Corn wouldn't even look at me. I didn't understand what the big deal was. "So he caught me masturbating. What's the big deal? Everybody has fantasies." I thought to myself.

"Hey guys. Sorry, I was acting a little moody yesterday. I wasn't myself. I've just had a couple things on my mind. I also got some bad news and didn't want to ruin everybody's day…my brother is in the hospital." Sylus said dropping himself into one of the bright orange chairs in the lobby.

"Oh man, I'm so sorry to hear that. What's wrong with him?" Corn asked. Rae stared down at her feet and didn't say a word. She showed no emotion whatsoever. We walked outside to the car.

"Sylvester apparently drank a little too much and threw himself in front of a truck. He's okay though. I'm not too worried about him anymore. They're going to release him in a couple of days. He'll be fine. It just kind of had me messed up yesterday…that along with some other things." Sy said looking over at me. It was hard for me to even look him in the face.

"Well, don't you think you should cut this trip short and go see him?" I asked giving him a hint that I didn't want him near me.

"Actually, no. I called him this morning. He's fine." Sy said spitefully smiling at me as we climbed into the black Ford Expedition.

"Okay, enough with the sad stuff. Let's hit this mall up. I got a couple of things I want to buy." Corn said mashing the gas and driving off.

We pulled up to the mall about twenty minutes later. "Sash and I are going to the DSW. We'll meet you in about an hour in the food court." Requelle said elbowing me in the ribs. She definitely had something up her sleeve. I just didn't know what it was yet. Rae didn't say a word to me as she walked me toward the mall exit.

"Rae, where are we going?" I asked.

"We're going back to the car. I've got to know what Sylus is keeping from me." She snapped. We walked out the exit door and to the parking lot. I stopped Rae mid step.

"Why go looking for something that you don't want to find? Why don't you just ask him what's on his mind? Maybe he'll tell you." I pleaded.

"No, Sash! I'm tired of being a fool and believing that this man actually tells me the truth! He's a liar and I know it!" She yelled.

"Okay, let's go then." I said finally giving up.

We jumped in the car, started the ignition and slammed on the gas. This woman was on a mission! I tried to talk to Rae the whole way back to the hotel to see what was going through her head but she wouldn't talk. I was trying so hard to understand why she was acting so strangely. We pulled up to the hotel in what seemed like ten seconds later. The slam of Requelle's door startled me.

"Sash come on! We don't have that much time." She yelled at me from outside the car.

I jumped out the car and ran for the entry door.

Once we finally got to the room, Rae began tearing up everything. She went through his bags, his planner, his palm pilot and finally went through his dirty clothes in the bathroom.

"*Ah Ha*! Found something!" She said with an unusual smile on her face.

"What is it?" I asked.

"It's a phone number!" She said as she ran for the hotel phone, picked it up and began dialing the mystery number.

"I don't think this is a good idea, Rae." I said biting my finger nails. Requelle waved her hand at me silently telling me to shut up. Rae put the phone on speaker phone.

"Hello?" The friendly light voice said.

"Hi. I found your phone number in my husband's pocket." She said calmly not jumping to any conclusions.

"Umm Hmm. Well, what's your husband's name?" She asked changing the tone in her voice. Requelle looked at me with her lips turned up as to say, "I told you so."

"His name is Sylus Videaux."

"Oh, yeah I know Sy. We had a real nice time the other night." The woman said with a giggle.

"Miss, what is your name?" Requelle asked standing to her feet.

"Dominique. And yours?" She asked sarcastically.

"Don't worry about what my name is *Bitch!* Were you aware that Sylus was married?"

"Yeah, he told me he was married. He said he wanted to have a good time. That's why he called me. Look chick, it doesn't matter to me whether my clients are married or not. I get paid to give men what they want. Your man wanted sex so I gave it to him! I'm just doing my job!" The whore yelled.

"What?! So…what? You're a …a prostitute or something?" Rae asked sitting back down on the bed and covering her mouth.

"I prefer the term *escort.* Look, Mrs. Videaux is it? Your husband paid me five hundred dollars for two hours of my time. He wanted me to give him his fantasy."

"And what was that?" Rae asked getting angry.

"Well…he wanted me to lick him from head to toe, ride him better than any other woman had before *including you,* and suck his long, thick black…"

Requelle slammed the phone down and fell to the floor. I sat right beside her and held her hand.

"A prostitute, Sash? I can't believe this! We are on vacation and he's doing this to me. I don't even know how to handle this. This man…this man…" She couldn't even get the words out of her mouth before she began crying and collapsing on the flower printed carpet. I felt so bad for her. I knew first hand how much of a dog Sylus was.

I laid on the floor with Requelle for what seemed like hours. She cried until finally she fell asleep. I looked down at my phone and realized that I had eighteen missed calls all from Cornelius and Sy. I stepped outside the hotel door and began dialing the numbers. I was startled by the loud slam of the elevator doors closing. Sy and Corn came storming down the narrow hallway like a two man herd of cows.

"Where were you guys?" Cornelius yelled down the hallway as he approached me. I just stood there looking down at a ketchup stain on my skirt. Corn stepped closer to me.

"Sasha, I asked you a question." He said repeating himself.

I finally looked up acknowledging that he was there. "We've been here the whole time."

"Why would you guys just leave us at the mall like that?" Sylus asked from behind Corn.

I just stood there.

"Baby, what's going on?" Corn asked grabbing my wrist and pulling me closer.

"Rae wanted to come back to the hotel to look for something and found out some bad news." I said glaring at Sylus mean as a snake.

Sylus walked over to me. "What are you talking about? What news?" He looked so concerned. He almost had me fooled.

"Your wife knows about your little date with *Dominique* the other night. I hope it was worth it." I said working my neck and snapping my fingers.

Sylus exhaled a deep sigh, pressed his body up against the clean white wall and fell to the floor. I could only imagine what was going through his head right now. He's probably feeling like a fool.

"Man, what were you thinking?" Corn asked.

Sy looked up at him. "I don't know, man. I…I guess I just wanted to have a good time and in the process I've screwed everything up. Man, honestly I just haven't been happy lately. Requelle hasn't been showing me any love and she's constantly accusing me of being unfaithful. I don't know why I did it. Maybe I was looking for a way out. I don't know. I didn't mean to hurt her though. I feel like such an idiot!" He said hitting himself in the forehead with the palms of his hands.

Corn sat on the floor next to him. "If you were having problems, you should have just went to her and talked to her about it. But it's too late for the shoulda coulda wouldas. You need to go in there and try to work this thing out if you really love her. Even if you don't want to be with her anymore, you at least owe her an explanation. She didn't deserve that from you, man."

"Corn, I know that! Like I said, I didn't mean to hurt her. I love her more than anything. I still want to be with her. I just needed a break. I know she's going to leave me. I don't even feel like dealing with this right now. I'll catch you guys later." Sy said picking himself up off the floor and walking away.

"I can't believe he's just going to walk away like that! He made his bed; he needs to lie in it! Aren't you going to stop him?" I asked throwing my hands up and getting into Corn's face.

He pushed my arms back down. "That has nothing to do with us. So no, I'm not going to do anything. We have to let them deal with their own issues." Corn said as he ushered me into the elevator.

We went to our room and watched a little TV. Corn eventually fell asleep, *as usual*. It seems like that's all he's been doing on this vacation. My phone began to vibrate. I looked down at my cell phone and saw that it was Sy. I debated whether or not I should pick it up. Before I had even come to a decision, my hands had already pressed the talk button.

"Hello?" I said clearing my throat.

"Hey. This is Sy."

"Hey. Where are you?"

"I'm down stairs in my car. Can you get out?" He asked.

I thought about it, looked over and Corn who was sleeping like an infant and finally responded. "Yeah, I can get out. Where are you parked?"

"Right outside your window. I'll see you in a minute." Sy said with exhaustion in his voice.

I sprayed myself with some perfume and made my way to the elevator. I finally made it to the first floor and began having second thoughts.

"Is this wrong?" I asked myself under my breath. I began walking to Sy's car against my better judgment. I saw smoke coming from the window and his long brown fingers waving at me through the crack. I walked over and got in the passenger's seat.

"Hey." He said looking over at me.

"Hey." I said being short with him.

"You don't mind if we drive somewhere do you?"

"No, I don't mind at all."

We drove to a park that was about fifteen minutes from the hotel. The park was completely empty. I was a little uncomfortable at first but eventually my discomfort went away. I almost felt like I was on a date or something. I swayed my head to the soft tunes of Musiq Soulchild.

"Are you mad at me?" He asked.

"No, why would I be mad at you? I'm *not your wife*."

"Because I cheated on Rae. Do you think I'm a dog?"

"Um…I really don't know how to answer that." I said scratching my scalp.

"Just tell me. I care about what you think." He said staring at me.

"Okay, yes. I think you're a dog that can't seem to control your dick!" I said with a smile on my face.

He laughed. "I can't believe you just said that to me! You know I've never cheated on Rae before now except for when I was messing with you…so wouldn't that make you a dog too?! *A female dog, right*?"

"No, you didn't! I never slept with you, Sy."

"So what? You don't have to sleep with somebody for it to be cheating. We've done everything except sleep together. We've kissed over a million times. We've touched and grabbed. And let's not forget about the night after we all graduated from college when you let me have a taste." He said licking out his tongue.

"Eeewww, nasty! Okay, I know I was wrong. That's why I'm not going there with you again." I said folding my arms.

"Oh, you're not? You sure about that? So why did you sneak out to be with me?" He asked pulling me closer.

I knew exactly where this was going but I didn't stop him. He pulled me closer and closer until I ended up in his lap with my legs straddled around his torso. I could smell the black and mild aroma coming from his warm smoke filled breath. He hugged me tight and stared into my green eyes.

"Do you still love me?" He asked bringing an arrogant smile to his face.

"I'm not answering that, *friend*." I said grabbing his face by his chin.

He began placing soft kisses on my neck.

"Sy, I can't." I managed to say even though it felt so good.

He continued kissing me like I hadn't even said anything.

"Let me have it." He demanded in a soft sexy voice. I was so turned on by him that I could no longer resist. He began unbuttoning my shirt.

"I love you, Sasha. Let me have it. Do you love me?" He asked in between kisses.

With each kiss I became more and more wet in my seat.

"Yes, I love you." I responded. Once those three little words came out it was a done deal. He snatched my shirt off and unsnapped my bra. I was so turned on by his aggression. He lifted my skirt, ripped off my panties and rammed himself inside of me like a raging bull. It hurt at first but eventually it was the best feeling that I had ever felt in my life. No one has ever made me feel this way. His penetration was uniquely satisfying just like in my fantasy. It was more than satisfying; it was earth-shattering.

In the midst of this encounter, I tried to convince myself to stop but I just couldn't. It felt too good. When we finally finished, we were both exhausted and our bodies were covered with little sweat droplets.

"No regrets, right?" Sy leaned over and said to me while trying to catch his breath.

"No." I responded.

I had just lied to him. The truth was I was full of regrets. What just went down could potentially ruin both of our marriages plus ruin my friendship with Rae. I don't know what I'll do if I lose the only friend I've ever known. I don't know what I'll do if I lose the only man who's ever loved me either. Corn is my world. How could I have done this to him?

We pulled back up to the hotel about ten minutes later.

"I'll see you tomorrow, Baby." Sy said opening up the car door for me.

"Ok. I'll see you then." I said walking into the hotel and getting in the elevator.

I slowly tip toed into my room to see if Corn was still asleep. He was knocked out. "I bet he didn't even realize I was gone." I whispered to myself. I slid into my pajamas and climbed into bed. I laid there stiff as a board. I couldn't get what had just happened out of my head. I kept replaying it over and over again. I was so full of mixed emotions. One part of me was excited and felt full of life. I felt like I was finally living my life to the fullest. But the other part of me was ashamed and afraid of what I had done. I was afraid of what Corn might do if he found out. I was afraid of how our lives would change if this devastating affair gets out. Sylus and I may have potentially ruined both of our lives for a mere hour of pleasure. *But what mind blowing pleasure it was.*

Chapter Six

"Purple Lace Panties"

"Baby, you need to wake up! It's 9:30. We were supposed to be at the airport already. Sash, get up!" Corn screamed at me.

"I am up, Corn. Leave me alone. All my stuff is packed I just gotta get dressed." I whined.

"Sash, I don't understand why you are so tired. We went to bed at like six o'clock last night. Maybe you got *too* much sleep. Get up!" He said hitting me with a pillow.

I finally picked myself up out of bed. I put on a soft pink sweat suit, tied my hair up in a pony tail, swished some mouthwash in my mouth and walked out the door. I felt so dirty inside that I didn't see any point in washing up.

"Okay Sy, that's the last bag." Corn said slamming the trunk door.

"Alright Man. Let me go tell Rae we're ready to go." He said whisking past me. I didn't even look in his direction.

Rae was still not talking to Sylus. She said she didn't want to address their drama until they got home. Rae came down, got in the truck and didn't utter a word. We got in the truck and were finally on our way to the airport. I noticed a change in Requelle's demeanor as she shifted in her seat.

"What the hell is this, Sylus?!!" She yelled.

"Baby, what are you talking about?" He said looking at her crazy. She picked up a pair of ripped panties with the tip of her index finger that she found underneath the passenger seat.

"You fucked that ho in the truck?! Are these Dominique's or someone else's?" She said in a low sarcastic voice. I looked up and saw that the purple lace panties she was holding were *mine*! I almost had a heart attack. I just knew that Rae was going to turn around and beat the hell out of me.

"No, I didn't have sex with her in the truck! They must have fallen out of my pocket. Baby, I'm sorry." Sy said looking back at me.

"So…what? You keep souvenirs of all the hoes you screw!? I hate you, Sylus!" Rae cried. Requelle slapped Sylus so hard that I thought his jaw was going to shatter and evaporate into thin air. I guess it felt good to take her anger out on him. She then balled up her fists and began fighting him. Sylus had to pull the car over just to restrain her. Sy finally had to get out of the car. He walked around to her side, pulled her out too and pinned her to the ground.

"This is getting ugly." Corn said looking at those two fools through the window.

"I know. You think we should call the police or something?" I asked.

"No, she needs to get that out before we get on the plane. If it gets bad, I'll go out there and break it up."

Corn picked up the panties from off the floor. He cocked his head sideways and stared at them for a few seconds.

"Sash." He said with his mouth hanging open.

"Yeah Babe. What is it?"

"Um…don't you have a pair of panties just like these?" He asked handing me the panties.

I didn't know what to say. My heart had just fallen into my stomach.

"Um…I don't think so…maybe." I said swallowing hard.

"No, you *DO* have a pair of underwear like these. You had them on yesterday. I remember because I'm the one that bought them for you for Valentine's Day last year."

By this time my heart was pounding. Corn ain't no fool so I knew he knew what was going on. Or at least I thought he did.

"Corn, I don't know. I don't remember what pair of underwear I wear each day. Are you accusing me of something?"

"Are you confessing to something? I hadn't accused you of anything. I just asked you a damn question." He said getting angry.

"Okay, yes I do have a pair of panties like those." I snapped.

"Are these yours?" He said leaning forward like he was about to jump me or something.

"NO! I'm not the only woman in the world with these kinds of panties! How could you ask me something like that, Corn?" I screamed trying to flip the script.

Corn got in my face. "Chill out! I'm done with this conversation."

The look on Corn's face told me that he knew something was shady. But he never said another word about it. Requelle and Sylus finally got back in the car. They were both tore up from the floor up. Sylus had scratches and bite marks all around his neck. He had blood coming out of his nose and his left ear. Requelle's hair was all over the place and she had leaves and branches stuck all in her shirt from being tied down to the ground. Nobody spoke a word the whole way to the airport.

Once we arrived at the airport, we all grabbed our things, boarded the plane and went back to Atlanta.

"Sash, I'm sorry about the later part of our vacation. I didn't mean to flip out like that. I'll make it up to you guys." She said giving me a hug and hopping into Sylus' navy blue Escalade.

"Don't even worry about it. I would have flipped out too, girl. I'm just sorry you had to go through that. What are you going to do?" I asked her through the parted window.

"I don't know, girl. I might just kill him." She said with a smirk on her face. For a minute there I thought she was serious.

"Bye, Rae." Corn yelled from across the parking lot.

"I'll see you later, Sasha." Sy said giving me a hug and a kiss on the cheek. This almost made me feel uncomfortable. No point in me feeling ashamed now, I've already done the deed and I can't take it back.

We finally got back home around eleven o'clock that evening. I wanted to tell Corn so bad what had happened the night before but I knew that I couldn't. I knew if I told that I would lose everything. I would have no reason to live after that. I love Corn so much. I never meant to hurt him like this. I don't know how I get myself in these predicaments. I thought once I graduated from college that these feelings for Sylus would go away. But I was wrong. My feelings for him now are much stronger than they ever were before. These feelings I have for Sylus are very real. I am in love with this man and I don't know how to get rid of it.

I decided to call my friend Sydnie. She always had such good advice. Ever since we were in school together she's always been the one that never made mistakes. We met several years ago and we're still friends to this day.

"Hey Girl!" Sydnie answered obviously looking at the caller ID.

"Hey Syd. It's so nice to hear your voice." I responded.

"It's nice to hear yours too. What's up?"

"How did you know that something was up?" I said with a frown on my face.

"Um…because you're calling me at damn near midnight. What's going on?" She asked sounding very serious.

"Syd, I've made a huge mistake. I…I…" I couldn't seem to get the words out.

"Sash, just tell me. You know that I'm not going to judge you. I love you and whatever you've done, I know it can be worked out. Tell me." She said trying to comfort me.

"I slept with Sylus." I belched out.

There was a long silence. "What!? How could you….wait…I don't mean to yell at you. How many times? Is this an isolated incident?" Syd asked trying to calm herself down.

"It happened last night. And yes that was the first time. I couldn't help it. He does something to me. I can't resist or avoid him, Syd.

I've been in love with him since college. I thought I was strong enough to…"

Syd interrupted. "What I don't understand is, if you know you have these feelings for him, why be around him so much? The four of you guys do everything together. That's what you get for playing with fire. You need to learn how to remove yourself from bad situations before they get worse. Stay away from him. Requelle is going to kill you. You know that, right?" She said with a giggle.

"Syd, don't say that! Man, I've made a mess and I don't know how I'm going to clean this up. What am I going to do, Syd?" I asked dropping my head.

"I don't know what to tell you. You were wrong, *dead wrong*. All you can do now is pray about this thing. Lord knows I've made my share of mistakes and one thing I've learned is God will always give you a way out if you trust Him and follow His direction." Sydnie said in a comforting voice.

Corn came walking around the corner. "Sash, it's late. Come to bed." He said rubbing his eyes. He always says that he sleeps better with me next to him.

I looked up at him. "Okay, I'll be off in a minute."

"Syd, I gotta go. I'll call you tomorrow, okay?" I said trying to avoid all of this Jesus talk.

"Sure, but remember what I said. I know you feel like you have nowhere to turn but God is always there even for those that don't accept Him. God reigns on the just as well as the unjust. You remember I said that, ok?"

"Okay. I'll talk to you later, Syd."

"Bye." She said hanging up the phone.

I jumped in bed with Corn and stared at him. He is so beautiful to me. I have a good man and Corn knows it. He's my everything; he completes me. I watched him sleep for another fifteen minutes and finally fell asleep.

Chapter Seven

"Running in the wrong direction"

Today is Sunday. I hate Sundays. Corn is trying to get me to go to church with him today but I don't think I'll be going. I can't stand church nor church folks. They ain't nothing but a bunch of hypocrites. They say one thing and do another. They condemn others for doing the same things they do when no one is watching. Church folks are always trying to teach somebody right and wrong when they know that they are the main ones sinning. *Shoot!* My last pastor's name was Pastor David E. Mayvis. I was nine years old. The name of his church was True Doers Baptist Church. I hated Pastor Mayvis. He was the biggest hypocrite and the biggest pervert that I had ever met in my life. Every Sunday morning in between Sunday school and morning worship service he would ask me to come into his office for prayer. He always said that he saw something in me that wasn't of God and that I needed extensive prayer. My mom would always agree and make me go in. I would go in and sit on one of the red velvet chairs. He would normally sit on his desk right in front of me and face me.

Pastor's Office
1989

"Hello there, little Sasha. How are you doing today?" Pastor Mayvis asked. I hated looking him in the face. His breath reeked of reefer and mouthwash. His face was black as lickerish and his teeth were so brown and rotted out that it looked like he had been chewing on links of shit his entire life. He wore the same wrinkled black suit and tie every Sunday.

"I'm fine." I said in a shy voice.

"Stand up, Sasha. I'm going to lay my hands on you and pray that demon out." He said motioning for me to get up and splattering spit in my face. He had a terrible lisp so he tended to spit when he spoke.

"Now lay right here on my desk." He said grinning.

I looked at him crazy. "Why?" I asked.

"You don't question God young lady! That's blasphemy! You can go to hell for that. You don't want to go to hell, do you? Now get up on this table like I told you to!" He said grabbing me by the arm and throwing me on the table. I ain't never read in the bible where it says you'll go to hell for questioning God. All I knew is that I definitely didn't want to go there. My mama told me that hell was a terrible place to go. She called it the eternal fire. I'd do anything to stay out of *the eternal fire*.

"Now, close your eyes. I don't want you to see the demon. If you look a demon in the eye, you could go blind." He said to me. He then taped my hands to the desk and covered my mouth with gray duck tape. Pastor Mayvis went over and locked his office door. He then slid his fat black hands up under my red and white plaid dress that my mom bought me for Easter that year. I wanted to scream but I couldn't. He rolled my underwear down and pried my legs open. The next few moments were treacherous, degrading and painful. With every pump I felt more and more helpless. He always told me that I was his special friend and that's why I get so much of his attention. Once he finally finished about twenty minutes later he picked my

Scooby-doo panties up off the floor and handed them to me. There were white splatters all over my shiny white church shoes.

"Put them on and don't tell anyone about our little secret. Remember you're my favorite little helper." He said as he watched me put my underwear back on as tears ran down my soft brown face. I never told a living soul. I was too embarrassed and ashamed. And for that reason, I hate church.

"Are you ready to go, Sash?" Corn asked standing at the front door with a frown of impatience.

"I don't think I can go, Corn. I…hate church. I…I…I just can't!" I said throwing my bible on the floor and plopping myself on the couch.

Corn came and sat next to me. "Baby, I know that you had some bad experiences when you were a little girl but you can't keep letting that control your life. Why won't you tell me what happened?" He asked.

"I don't want to talk about it, Corn."

"I thought we told each other everything? Please tell me so that I can understand." He pleaded.

I took a deep breath and closed my eyes. "Okay. When I was nine… my pastor… raped me. He raped me over and over again. I won't go, Corn." I cried.

Corn's mouth flung open. He placed his hand over it. "I didn't know that, Sash. I am so sorry that that happened to you. How many times did that happen?" He asked putting his head down.

"More times than I can remember. He did it every other Sunday until I was eleven." I said with a frown on my face and a heart full of pain and hate.

"Wow, I don't know what to say, Sash. I'm so sorry you had to go through that." He said putting his arms around me.

"There's nothing to say. Church folks ain't nothing but a bunch of hypocrites. And preachers are perverts." I yelled getting up off the couch.

"So you think I'm a hypocrite?"

"No, I don't. But a lot of Christians are and I don't feel like fooling with them or God right now."

"Don't you understand that you need God more than anything now? You don't go to church for church folks. You go to church to worship and praise God. I really want you to come to church with me this Sunday. If you go this Sunday, I promise I won't ask you to go again. *Please?*" He said getting on his knees and begging me like a little puppy. I couldn't say no to those big puppy dog eyes so I agreed to go ahead and go.

I've known Corn for almost thirteen years and I've never gone to church with him even once. I don't know why it was so detrimental for me to go *this Sunday*. We arrived at the House of Praise Fellowship Church about fifteen minutes before the service started. We walked in. I felt turbulence in the pit of my stomach. The church was beautiful on the inside. It seated maybe twelve hundred people. There was bright red carpet under my feet and an auditorium full of wooden stained pews.

"Baby, I want you to meet my pastor. This is Pastor Harvey. Pastor, this is my beautiful wife, Sasha." Corn said grabbing my hand.

"It is so nice to finally meet you. I've heard so many wonderful things about you. You have a good man standing here beside you. He is a true man of God and I see wonderful things happening to him in the near future." The pastor said shaking my hand.

This pastor looked nothing like Pastor Mayvis. He was tall, slim and handsome. He had on a navy blue pinstriped suit with navy blue snake skinned shoes. He had on a clean crisp white shirt and a navy blue tie. His skin was a caramel color and his teeth were white as winter. He had big teddy bear medium brown eyes and a very well groomed goat tee. His voice was smooth as velvet. There was something about his voice that calmed me. When I shook his hand I could feel such a spirit about him that it was scary.

"Hi, it's nice to meet you Pastor Harvey." I responded.

"It is nice to meet you too, Sister Sasha." Pastor Harvey walked down to the Pulpit to get ready for morning worship. Corn walked me to a pew that was right up in front. *He said he wanted me close to the fire.* I don't know what it was about this church but something made me feel so at home even though I haven't attended church in almost fifteen long years.

Morning worship was awesome. Everybody was standing up clapping and singing. It seemed as though everyone was having so much fun and was so spirit filled. It was nothing like this at True Doers. The choir did their thing too. They almost got *ME* excited. I didn't recognize the songs that they sang since I don't listen to gospel music but they were very beautiful and peppy. They sang a song that said, "You came from Heaven to earth to show the way, from the earth to the cross my debt you paid." For some reason that song gave me goose bumps. It made me begin to believe that God has already wiped away my sins. But I don't believe that. Why would God do that for a mere sinner like me? I'm in too deep.

After the choir sang, it was time for altar call. Corn walked me up to the front of the altar for prayer. The pastor prayed himself into a sweat. I really wasn't listening until the pastor came from behind the pulpit and touched my forehead with an oily finger.

"Lord, help this child! Satan wants her, Lord. Please God deliver her from bondage. Set her free! Satan can't have her! She needs a breakthrough, God!" He yelled at me. He had such a tight grip on my head that it made me dizzy. Before I knew it about ten people had surrounded me. They all had a hand on me. I felt so uncomfortable. "Do they think that I'm a demon or something?" I thought to myself. I looked over at Corn and he was in tears with his hands lifted up to the sky. The sister behind me screamed at the top of her lungs and fell to the floor. That scared the hell out of me. I didn't know what was going on. Nobody in the room seemed to notice that this woman had just fainted.

After the prayer period was finally over, it was time for the sermon. I forget which book it came out of but it was about knowing the difference between guilt and conviction. Pastor Harvey said that guilt is not of God and it will completely break you down and tare you up. Conviction comes from the love of God. It sounded like a bunch of mumbo jumbo to me.

After the sermon it was time for invitation to discipleship. I felt like Pastor Harvey was talking directly to me.

"Someone in here is hurting. Someone in here is confused and in a bad situation. All you have to do is surrender it all over to Jesus. He will take the weight off your shoulders, Child. Just surrender to Jesus! He's waiting for you at the altar. He's waiting! He's saying come, my child. He loves you. You are leading yourself into a path of destruction. God doesn't want that. He loves you, Beloved." He cried in the microphone. Everything in me was telling me to just get up from my seat and walk up to the altar but something was holding me back. My heart felt so heavy. I knew he was talking to me but I couldn't move. My legs were so heavy they felt like they were being held down by chains and shackles. I began to cry. Corn looked over at me and hugged me close. He saw that I was struggling. I snatched away from Corn and finally was able to lift myself from the wooden pew but instead of going to the altar where I was called, I turned around and walked out the door. I looked back and saw Corn slumped over in his seat on the verge of tears. I didn't know what I was running from but I knew that I was running.

Corn caught up with me in the parking lot. He grabbed me from behind and whispered in my ear. "I know you're hurting. I know you feel like it is impossible for you to put your past to rest. I have a past too, Sasha. I was apart of one of the most deadly gangs in the nation. I should have been dead a long time ago. In fact, I would have been dead a long time ago but God had his hand on my life. I was a bad man and if I can overcome that path of destruction, I know that you can too. We all have a purpose here. God saved me and I know he can save you too. You just have to give him complete control. Don't turn your back on God like this. He has too much invested in you. He loves you."

I turned around and faced him. "Corn, I don't even know who I am anymore. I've been so consumed with my problems and my past that I've lost myself and I can't find Sasha. I'm lost, Corn. *You* don't even know the *real* me because I don't even know the *real* me. Corn, I don't deserve you. I don't deserve God."

Cornelius seemed so shocked at what I had just said. He just stood there with a frown on his face.

"None of us deserve God, Sasha. None of us are worthy. But that just goes to show you how good God is. If you can't praise Him for anything else, praise Him for that! I understand why you believe you don't deserve God because every Christian in the world believes that. But why do you believe that you don't deserve me?"

I dropped my head down. "I've done some bad things and I'm not a good person."

I put both my hands over my face and cried. I wanted to tell Corn everything that I've ever done to betray him but the words wouldn't come out of my mouth.

Corn pulled my hands off my face.

"What are you talking about?" He asked.

"I can't tell you. Just leave it alone. Can we go home now?" I asked taking the keys out of Corn's pocket.

He looked at me like he wanted to cry. "Okay, we can go home if that's what you want. I have to be honest, I don't know how we've made it this long if you haven't even been honest with me. I was not even aware that you had been keeping secrets from me until today. You know everything about me. How come I don't know everything about you?" He asked.

"Because if you did, you would hate me."

"No, I wou…"

"Let's just go." I said cutting him off mid sentence.

We got in the car and drove home. Corn didn't speak to me the whole ride home. I guess that's definitely understandable. He's right; he doesn't know anything about me except for what's on the surface. Maybe I'm afraid that he won't love the real me. Now that I've betrayed him in the worst way possible, I know that he will hate me. I know he's going to leave me if he finds out about Sylus. I don't know what to do. I have nowhere to turn. I don't want to lose my husband. He is the best thing that has ever happened to me. I know no one will probably understand why I appear to love my husband so much and yet I'm creeping with his best friend. Believe me; I don't understand it either.

Chapter Eight

"Another fight, another lose"

I haven't spoken to Sylus since the vacation almost three months ago. I've spoken to Rae a couple times. She has pretty much cut herself off from the world. I don't know if she's embarrassed about her husband cheating on her time and time again or if she just wants some time to herself. She's been acting very strange since the trip so I don't invade her space too much.

Corn is in Dallas this week on a business trip. He's a much respected dentist with one of the most respected dental companies in Atlanta. There was a loud knock at the door. I went over to open it. I looked through the peep hole and saw that it was Sylus. I stood there for a second and finally opened the door.

"Hey Sasha." He said pushing himself in.

I shut the door behind him. "Hey Sy. What are you doing here?"

"I just wanted to see how you were doing, I guess." He smiled at me.

"Yeah, well they have phones for that. You *know* Corn is out of town. What are you really doing here?" I said folding my arms across my chest.

"Sash, stop trippin. Come sit by me. I really just want to talk. Is that okay?"

I stared at him and finally went and sat down next to him.

"What do you want to talk about?" I said already knowing the answer.

"Let's talk about us. Tell me how you feel about me." He said scooting closer to me.

"Why?" I snapped.

"Because I want to know. I've risked everything for you."

"Sy, I just don't want to talk to you about that. What we did was a mistake and it shouldn't have happened. You're right; we risked everything for a few moments of pleasure. Don't you love your wife?" I asked sincerely.

"Yes, Oprah. I do love my wife. But I love you too. I've loved you for many years. Sometimes I wish that I had met you before I met Rae. I know I can make you happy. I don't know why I love you so much but I do. I'm sorry. These last three months have been killing me because I haven't been able to see or talk to you. Rae tells me everyday how much she hates me. I don't know how much longer I'm going to be able to put up with that."

"Sylus, I love my husband and I don't want to lose him because of a few horny moments." I said rolling my eyes.

"Believe it or not, I love your husband too. He's my best friend. I know when nobody else has my back that he will. I care about Corn too, Sash. I don't want to hurt him. I promise I don't. I really wish that I could just forget about you but I can't." He said standing to his feet.

"Why are you telling me all of this, Sy?" I asked.

"I just wanted to let…."

"What, do you think by you saying all of this that I'm going to sleep with you again? Is that it?" I rudely interrupted and stood to my feet.

"Sweetheart, I'm not trying to run game on you. I really just…"

"Whatever! I don't want to hear anything that you have to say. *You're full of shit!* I'm not doing this with you again!" I interrupted again.

Frustrated, Sylus walked over to me, grabbed me by the shoulders and shook me. "Sasha, will you just listen for one gotdamn minute?!"

I just stood there.

"I am not trying to hurt you or get in between your legs or anything like that. I just wanted you to know what was going on in my head right now. I wanted to know how you felt about me. I could have stayed at home for this shit!" He said letting go of me.

I didn't know what had just happened but I was starting to feel a familiar arousal. My heart began to pump and my breathing became irregular. I could no longer retrain or control myself. I practically jumped him. He was so shocked and confused by my actions. But he totally embraced it. We rolled around on the floor for at least two hours. We lied there butt naked on the light blue carpet covered in sweat. That was the best sex I had ever had. For the first time in my life I became the aggressor.

"I thought we weren't going there again?" Sy asked sarcastically.

"I didn't want to but like I said before; you make me break all my rules. I don't know what you do to me." I said looking in his eyes.

"Do you love me?" He asked stroking my hair.

"Yes I do." I responded looking away from him.

He grabbed me and pulled me closer to him. "You ready for round two, Baby?" He asked giving me a passionate kiss. He already knew the answer to that.

Sylus finally left and went back home after round six. He worked me like no other brotha ever had before. I think I may be addicted or maybe I'm sick. In the heat of the moment I never feel any regrets nor do I feel any guilt but after the fact, I feel terrible; so terrible that I can't stand to look at myself in the mirror. Sometimes I feel so guilty that I can't even function from day to day. I can't go a day, an hour or even a minute without thinking about Sylus and this passionate love we share. I don't know how I've dug myself this hole but each day it gets deeper and deeper. Sooner or later I know my sins are going to push me in and bury me. I don't know how I'm going to look Corn in the face. I know it's only a matter of time before I crack.

"Hey, Babe, I'm home. Are you here?" Corn asked as he dropped his luggage on the bedroom floor.

I came flying out the bathroom. "Hey Baby. You're back early. How was your trip?"

He looked so good in his black slacks, black polo shirt and his creamy tan cashmere coat.

"It was so dull but I learned a lot of interesting stuff though so it was informative. The conference was over today and tomorrow was just the faculty party so I decided to come home early." He said laying his long body across the bed.

"Oh, well that's good. Did you miss me?" I asked with a fake smile on my face.

He climbed off the bed and walked over to me. "Of course I did. You're my sweet lady." He whispered in my ear giving me a warm hug and a kiss on the lips.

I just wanted to cry.

"What's wrong, honey?" He asked wiping a tear from my cheek.

"Oh…nothing. I just really love you. You know that right?"

"Of course, silly." He said laughing at me. He slid his hands up under my shirt and began fondling my breast.

"*Oh no, not tonight! Please, not tonight.*" I thought to myself.

Corn began kissing my neck and pulling my shirt off. I felt so gross. I probably still had Sylus' juices inside of me. I didn't know what else to do so I started gagging.

"Sasha, what's wrong?" Corn asked.

I didn't respond. I just pushed him out the way, ran into the bathroom and shut the door.

"Sasha? Are you okay?" Corn yelled through the door.

"I…I think I'm sick." I said gagging and flushing the toilet at the same time.

Corn finally got sick of waiting and peeked his head in the door. I was humped over the toilet like a fool looking very ill.

"Sasha, are you okay? You seemed fine when I first got here. What's wrong, Baby?" He walked over closer to me, kneeled down and picked my face up out of the toilet.

"I'm fine. I just need to take a shower and go to sleep. I had a long day today."

Corn said okay and turned the shower on. He picked me up off the floor and laid me on the bed. He undressed me and I then got up and got in the shower. As I began washing Sylus off of my body I noticed Corn had come in.

"Baby, do you feel any better?" He asked.

"Oh, I feel a lot better." I responded.

Before I could even get the words out good, Corn had climbed into the shower with me.

"What are you doing?" I asked with an uneasy smile on my face and an uncomfortable giggle. Corn totally ignored me and grabbed me by the waist. He pressed my body up against his and passionately stuck his tongue in my mouth. He ran his hands down to my round bottom and squeezed it tight. I felt like such a whore. He picked me up by my legs and straddled them across his torso. I would've just faked an orgasm but he always knows when I'm faking. He finally finished about twenty five minutes later. I was so relieved.

Once I got dressed, laid down in our king size bed and closed my eyes Corn thumped me on the shoulder.

Please don't tell me he wants a round two. Please don't!

"What is it?" I asked turning around and looking at Corn. The expression on his face had me worried. I could literally see the anger eroding from his face.

"What is this?" He said pointing at the back side of my neck. I got up and ran to the mirror to see what he was talking about.

Oh, my God! It's a passion mark!

My heart was beating a thousand times a minute. "I don't know. What does it look like?" I said scared to death.

He sat up on the bed staring at me like a raging bull.

"It looks like a hickey. Is there something you want to tell me?" He asked in a surprisingly calm voice like he already knew that I had been creeping.

"What? What do you mean *do I have something that I want to tell you?*" I said turning around and facing him. He got up off the bed and grabbed me by the face.

"Don't play games with me! Be a woman and tell me the truth for once!" He said staring right into my eyes.

"What do you mean *for once?*" I asked folding my arms.

"Are you screwing around on me, Sasha?"

"What?"

"Sasha! Are you cheating on me?! Just answer the damn question and stop playing games with me."

I didn't answer. I just stood there in total shock. I finally built up enough courage to just tell him.

"Corn...I...I..."

"You know what? I'm overreacting. I know you love me, Baby. I'm just trippin'. Maybe I'm tired from the plane ride or something. I didn't mean to come home and attack you like this. I'm sorry. I know you're not cheating on me. Do you forgive me?" He said interrupting me.

I didn't know what else to say except, "Of course I forgive you, Baby. You're just tired. You need to get some rest." I walked over to his side of the bed and put the covers over him. He fell asleep about five seconds later. He must have been really tired. I know my man isn't stupid. I don't know why he just let it go. Maybe he just didn't want to believe that the mark on my neck was *actually* a passion mark. I almost wish that I had confessed. At least then I could have gotten some relief. I felt so terrible about what I had done. I wish I could take it all back but I can't.

Chapter Nine

"Will this nightmare ever end?"

Corn and I got married five years ago on today. I can remember our beautiful wedding like it was yesterday. Our colors were royal blue, yellow and white. Cornelius was so gorgeous that day. He had on a white tux trimmed in royal blue silk and a royal blue tie. My dress was pure white. It was strapless with a twenty foot train and the back was out. I wore my hair up in a ponytail with loose curls hanging down. I felt so beautiful that day. And what made it extra special was that my grandmother on my mother's side was still alive. She let me where a pair of her diamond stud earrings. Those earrings had been in the family for many generations.

Up until about five months before my wedding I was so angry with my grandmother for not taking me in when my mother died. I didn't understand why she didn't want me. It wasn't until later that she told me she had colon cancer and only six months to live. She told me that she didn't want me to have to suffer another lose nor did she want me to be thrown away to someone else. Her name was Maple

Lee Symmons. She was the only family member that I believe truly loved me. I miss her so much. She was the only member of my family that ever sent me birthday or Christmas cards. She was the only one that gave me any kinds of gifts. She was also the only family member that attended my wedding and college graduation. Granny was the only person that gave a damn. Sometimes it really hurts but other times I'm just glad that at least one person cared. She was the only reason that I was able to go to college. She wrote me a check for fifty thousand dollars to send me to the school of my choice. And when she died four years ago she left me three hundred thousand dollars in life insurance. She used to tell me when I was a little girl, "Granny will always take care of you no matter what happens." She was right and she kept her promise.

We're having our anniversary party tonight at Club Blue. Club Blue is one of the finest jazz clubs in town. They're sold out every weekend. Corn has invited at least a hundred people to this party. He invited a lot of his family and several of his friends including Sylus. I only invited three people, Sydnie, Kevin and Requelle. And honestly, I'm not even sure Sydnie and Kevin are coming. Rae came early to help me with decorations.

"Girl, this party is going to be the bomb! Aren't you exited?" She said trying to blow up a balloon.

"I mean, I guess." I shrugged.

"You need to loosen up, girl. What's wrong? This is supposed to be a fun day for you." She said giving up on the balloon.

"I don't know. I just hate attending parties where I don't know anybody. This is basically a family reunion for Corn. This has nothing to do with me. This is *his* party not *mine*." I said sitting next to her.

"What? How could you say that? This is your wedding anniversary party. It's all about you."

"No, it's not. His family doesn't even like me. In fact, they hate me." I said wiping a tear from my face.

Rae frowned at me. "How do you know that?"

"At our wedding, Cortney, Corn's mom, came up to me right before it was time for me to march down the aisle and said that she wished Corn had never met me."

"What? I cannot believe that! Did you tell Corn what she said?" She asked gasping for air.

"No, I didn't want to start any trouble and plus Corn thinks his mom adores me. Yeah right. He is so blind or at least he pretends to be."

Requelle and I continued making the decorations when we noticed a very strange gentlemen standing outside the bar. This man was a very handsome older man maybe in his late forties or early fifties. He was light skinned with very pretty short curly hair and green eyes. He had on a navy blue business suite and a white collar shirt. He was standing by the window looking right at me. I thought maybe he was lost or something but at the same time I was too afraid to go out there and ask him.

"Sash, who is that guy? He is *f-i-n-e*!" Rae said snapping her fingers with every letter.

"I don't know. He looks very familiar though." I said squinting my eyes at him.

"Sasha, he looks just like you."

That's when it dawned on me. That strange looking man outside was *my father*! I immediately went into an internal panic. My heart was thumping so fast that I thought I was about to have a stroke.

"What's wrong with you? Do you know that guy or something?" Rae asked grabbing my hands trying to keep them from shivering. Before I could even answer her I fell to the floor and woke up in the emergency room.

"What happened?" I asked rubbing my eyes.

"You fainted. Do you feel okay?" Corn asked stroking my cheeks.

"Corn? Hey, Baby. What are you doing here? I thought you had to pick up your folks from the airport." I asked with a confused expression on my face.

Corn laughed at me. "I did. Two days ago."

A wave of laughter filled the room. I was so confused. I took a look around the room and realized that I was surrounded by at least twenty people.

"What? How long have I been sleeping?" I asked.

"About two days. The doctor said your blood pressure was dangerously high so he kept you here a couple of days."

"Oh no, I missed our anniversary party. I'm so sorry, Corn!" I screeched as I sat up on the twin size hospital bed. When I sat up, I began identifying who all was in the room. Most of them were Corn's family and friends. I was really surprised that they even cared enough to come visit me.

"Are you feeling okay, Sweetie?" Corn's mom asked peeking her head in between Rae and Corn.

Like you give a damn!

"Yeah, I'm fine. Thank you."

"We've rescheduled the party for tomorrow night. You think you will be feeling better by then?" Corn asked.

"Yeah, I'll be fine. I wouldn't miss it for the world.

        The hospital released me about five or six hours later. I was still in shock from what I had seen the other day. I hadn't seen my daddy since I was seven years old, over twenty years ago. What made him want to come back now? I hope he doesn't think that he's still my daddy.

"How dare he try to come back and see me?! He got me all worked up and got me sitting up in the hospital and shit! I hate him!" I yelled to myself.

"Sasha, what are ranting and raving about?" Sylus asked. Corn invited Rae and Sy over for dinner to keep me company. He thought I would enjoy their company.

"Where's Rae and Corn?" I asked looking around the room.

"Corn went to the store to pick up a few things for the party tomorrow and Rae went to go get you guys' anniversary present. Corn didn't want you here by yourself so he asked me to stay and look after you." He said with a smile.

"I don't want you here Sy." I frowned.

"Why?" He asked walking over to the bed I was laying in.

"Because, I can't do this anymore! I can't keep betraying Corn like this. I want "you and me" to stop! I don't think I can take this anymore, Sy. I don't trust myself around you."

"I thought you loved me?"

"Sylus, I do. Look, I can't do this right now. I have a lot on my mind right now. Please just….." I said with a sigh.

"Okay, I love you too. So how the hell do you expect me to just leave you alone after we've had sex countless times for the past year? How can you expect me to just stay away from you? Honestly, I don't see any point in stopping *now*. We've already messed up and us cleaning it up ain't gone take away the years of dirt we've been bathing in!" He said grabbing my hand.

I didn't know what to do. I really wanted everything to just stop. I wish I had never even gotten involved with this man. *"I feel like such a fool!"* I thought to myself. How did I get myself into this mess?

"Sasha… are you listening to me? I *am* talking to you, right?" He said with a whole lot of attitude.

"Sy, you heard what I said. I want you to leave my house right now! I want you to get away from me!" I screamed.

"Oh, now you don't want me near you, huh? You weren't saying that when I was fucking your brains out! You weren't saying that when I had you sneaking out to be with me! You weren't saying that when…"

"Sy just shut up! I don't want to hear this shit!"

"Why because I'm telling you the truth? The truth hurts, huh?" He smirked at me.

I jumped up off the bed and began walking toward the front door. Sy followed closely behind me and grabbed me by the waist. "Let go of me!" I yelled at him trying to break away from his hold. He picked me up and threw me back on the bed.

"Sy, please just leave me alone! I don't want to do this anymore!" I said yelling and crying at the same time. He totally ignored me as he ripped my shirt and bra off. I kicked, screamed and scratched but it didn't help one bit. He leaned down and whispered in my ear. "Why are you fighting me? You know you don't want me to stop. I love you. I'm never letting you go." It scared the hell out of me the way he said that. He pinned my arms down with one hand and tore my panties off with the other one. He then forced himself inside of me. All I could do was cry while he took what he wanted. I felt so helpless. I couldn't believe Sylus was doing this to me. He then flipped my body over and rammed himself in my rear. I felt so violated as he aggressively pulled my hair. He treated me like I was a two dollar hooker that he picked up of the street. This felt nothing like it did when we made love. When we made love it was passionate, exciting and dangerous.

"Sylus please stop. Please…" I whimpered.

"Okay, I'll stop." He whispered as he gave me one last hard pump and a kiss on the back. His sweaty torso collapsed on top of my helpless body. After a few seconds I felt a warm substance squirt and drip on my back. I wanted to vomit.

"Do you still love me?" He whispered in my ear. I laid there stiff as a bored. I could feel his hot smoke filled breath penetrating ear and covering my neck. It sent uncomfortable chills up my spine.

He picked himself up, went into the living room and turned on the television. I was lying in the bed as if he was still lying on top of me. I just laid there crying and wondering why he had just done that to me. I finally built up enough strength to pull myself up out of bed. I picked my torn up clothes off the floor and went into the bathroom. I stared at myself in the mirror for about thirty minutes and I suddenly felt my insides eroding upward. I ran over to the toilet and threw up all of my pain and anger. It hurt so bad. I flushed the toilet and jumped in the shower. I scrubbed so hard that the clear water dripping at my feet became bloody. I felt like I had been ripped from head to toe. I finally collapsed onto the blue tile shower floor and fell asleep.

"Sasha!" Corn yelled hysterically.

I looked up and saw the fright in his face. "I'm fine. I just fell asleep." I said in a quiet scratchy voice. Corn tried to convince me to go back to the hospital but I refused. He stepped into the shower and picked my wet bloody body up off the floor and sat me on the toilet. He dried me off and put my soft pink robe on my shivering body.

"Sasha…please tell me what's going on. Where is Sylus?" Corn asked as he picked me up and put me on the bed that I had just been raped on. I immediately felt ill.

"Can you please lay me in the guest room?" I asked looking up at Corn. He didn't understand that at all but he didn't ask any questions.

He kept asking me what had happened but I really didn't know what to tell him. I just sat there staring into space like a crazy person.

"Sasha, talk to me." He pleaded.

"I don't want to talk about it, Corn. Please just let me be."

He laid down beside me and waited until I appeared to be sleep.

Once he thought I was sleep, he walked into the living room and began yelling at Sylus.

"Sy where were you? I asked you to watch over Sash while I was gone! What happened to her?" Corn yelled.

"Man, I don't know. I went in the room with her and she starting screaming at me telling me to get out! What was I supposed to do?" Sy yelled back throwing his hands up.

Damn Liar!

"Whatever, man! I don't mean to yell at you. I'm just worried, okay?" Corn said throwing himself on the couch next to Sy.

"Yeah, I know. We cool though. I know you're a little stressed out right now." Sylus said patting Corn on the knee.

Bastard!

I couldn't believe how that niggah was just sitting there lying right in Corn's face. But I guess we're both guilty of that. Maybe I'm just as guilty as he is, *if not more*. I just want this nightmare to end.

Chapter Ten

"The cat had left the bag"

The party was starting in twenty five minutes and I still hadn't even picked myself up out of bed. I could hear Sylus in the living room laughing and playing like nothing ever happened. *I can't believe him!* Does he really think that I wanted him to do that to me? Does he really think that I wanted him to rape me and then cum on me like I'm a freaking whore? Does he really think that?! What happened to the man that I was just so in love with that I was willing to risk everything? I wondered what happened to the man that used to make me feel so free and excited. What happened to the man that made me laugh and giggle? I mean Sylus was so special to me. He would say all the right things and touch me in all the right places. No man could turn me on the way that Sylus did. He was the only man who could make me cry when we were making love. He was the only man who could blow me a kiss that would send electrified currents up my spine. I just don't understand all of this. How could I have been so blind?

I finally stopped my whining, threw myself out of bed, wiped all the tears from my tear stained caramel cheeks and got dressed. I knew I had to put on a really good front if I wanted to fool anybody. I put on my pink slacks with the cuff in the bottom, a white turtle neck sweater and my hot pink pumps. I wore my hair down and let loose curls cuff my slender face. I went over to the mirror and stared at my dried up face for about five minutes. I then picked up a tube of rosy pink lipstick that I found at the bottom of my bathroom drawer and rubbed it on my lips. I was finally ready to entertain.

I walked out into the midst of the one hundred people that were sitting around in my living room. I took a big breath of clean air and I was ready to go.

"What are y'all doing sitting around? This is a party, is it not?" I said pulling people out of their seats and turning the CD player on. I got a couple of the men to help me move the couches, tables and chairs.

"Let's party!" I said cranking up the volume. Everybody thought I was being so funny but they eventually got up and started dancing.

"May I have this dance?" Corn asked performing the corniest royal bow that I had ever seen.

"Why of course, sailor." I laughed.

Dancing with Corn was like a much needed breath of fresh air. He smelled so good and he felt good too. It seemed like he hadn't held me like this in ages. I felt so safe in his arms. He looked down at me and gave me a slow passionate kiss. I wanted to eat him up.

"I love you so much, Sasha." He said in a Barry White voice.

"I love you too; more than anything and everything in this whole world." I said looking up at his perfect face. He gave me a beautiful smile from ear to ear.

"Tell me what happened this afternoon. It's killing me not knowing." He said staring at me.

"I really don't want to talk about it Corn. I...I promise I will tell you everything when the time comes. I promise I will. Okay?" I said almost afraid that I had even said that much.

"Okay. If that's what you want then I have to respect that. But I have to be honest. I'm really getting tired of you keeping secrets from me."

"I know. I'm sorry. I won't keep anything else from you ever again. I'll tell you whatever you want to know. But for now, let's enjoy our party." I said giving him a peck on his soft pink lips.

We danced for what seemed like hours staring in each other's eyes. When we broke from each other's gaze we realized that we were the only ones dancing. Everybody else was over at the table eating up all our food.

"Woman, you threw down! These lemon pepper wings are off the chain!" Bobby said licking lemon pepper sauce off his fingers. Bobby is Corn's younger brother from Virginia. He's a freshman at Howard University. He is one of the smartest most mature young men that I have ever met. He got into Howard on a full music scholarship. He looks just like his big brother too. He's a cute little thing.

"Thanks, Bobby. I'll send some home with you."

A big smile appeared on his face. "Oh, thank you. Big bro you got yourself a good woman here."

"Of course. Could it be any other way?" Corn said being cocky.

"Corn, can I borrow your wife for a minute?" Sylus asked tapping Corn on the shoulder.

Hell no! I think you've borrowed me enough for the day!

"Yeah, man of course you can. Don't be too long though. We're about to open the gifts."

Sy walked me into the game room.

"What?" I snapped and folded my arms in front of my chest.

"Sasha, I'm sorry about what happened. I didn't mean to hurt you. I was just …"

"You didn't mean to hurt me? When I say no, I mean NO!" I yelled and turned away from him.

"Baby…"

"I'm not your *baby!*" I yelled at him.

"Sasha, keep your voice down." He whispered at me.

"You know what? I'm about ready to just tell Corn and Rae everything! I'm tired of all of this secrecy! I'm about to explode, Sylus. I can't take this anymore. You say you love me and all of that mushy shit but you sure have a funny way of showing it!" I cried.

"Tell Rae and Corn what?" Rae asked walking around the corner scaring the hell out of both of us.

"Hey Baby. How long were you standing there?" Sylus asked with a shaky voice.

Rae put her hand on her hip. "Long enough. Now, answer my question."

"It's nothing…Rae…it's nothing." Sylus replied. I stood there and said nothing but my heart was beating a million times a minute. I felt like my legs were going to give out on me at any moment.

"Don't tell me *it's nothing*!" Rae yelled.

"Baby, please calm down. Let's not do this here." Sylus said walking over to her and putting his arms around her.

"I will not *calm down!* You two have been acting funny for the past couple of months and I want to know what the fuck is going on! Now!!!" Rae screamed.

By this time, all the guests knew something had happened and they politely said goodnight and showed themselves to the door. Corn came walking around the corner.

"What the hell is going on here?" Corn asked full of frustration.

"I don't know; ask Sy and your wife." Rae said pointing at me.

"Sash?" Corn said staring at me.

"Rae, can we please do this at home?" Sylus pleaded.

"Sasha, what's going on?" Corn asked me with a frown on his face. He came over and grabbed my hands. Then he looked over at Sylus and saw the guilt written all over his face.

"Sylus?" Corn said looking over at him.

Sylus looked at me and mouthed the words, "I'm sorry."

What is he about to do?

"Corn you know that you're my best friend. And I love you like a brother." Sylus said taking a big breath.

Corn put a frown back on his face and put his thick hands on his hips. "I know that but why are you telling me this, man?

Sylus stuck his hands in his blue jean pockets. "Corn, I'm in love…with Sasha."

"What?" Requelle yelled in a high pitched voice.

Corn walked over closer to him and got right in his face.

"I'm going to need you to say that one more time." Corn said as he balled up his fists and stuck them by his sides.

"Corn...man...I'm sorry. I don't know how this happened. But I love Sasha. I've loved her since college." He belched out in one scared breath.

Corn turned and looked at me. "Did you sleep with him, Sasha?"

"Corn, I'm sorry. Baby, I didn't mean to...."

"Did you sleep with him? I don't want to hear all that other shit! Answer my question!? Corn yelled at me.

"Yes." I answered.

By this time, my face was covered in tears and regrets.

Before I could even get an explanation out, Corn had balled up his fists and socked Sylus right in the jaw. Sy fell to the floor.

"Corn please calm down." Sylus said holding his jaw in place.

"How many times did you sleep with my wife, Sylus? How many times!" Corn yelled. His yell was so full of anger that it almost sounded like a lion's roar.

"I don't know."

"You don't know, huh? How long?"

"About a year."

"*WHAT!*" Corn yelled.

"I can't believe this shit! Sasha, a year? You were supposed to be my girl. We were more than girls! We were sisters! I thought you loved me?" Requelle yelled.

"Rae, I'm sorry. I don't know how this got so out of control." I said weeping.

"Save it!" She yelled at me.

"Baby, I'm sorry that I've hurt you. I'm sorry." Sylus managed to say.

"Oh, you're not sorry yet but you *WILL* be! Get up off the floor and get your ass in the car!" Rae demanded. She picked her purse up off the floor and walked right out the front door.

"Corn, I'm sorry man." Sylus said picking himself up off the floor and walking out behind Rae.

Corn looked over at me, turned around and walked down the hall into our bedroom. I followed closely behind him. I tried to talk to him but he wasn't trying to hear anything that I had to say. He just kept asking me why. I didn't have an answer for that.

"How many times, Sash?" He asked plopping himself down on the bed.

"I don't know. A lot...I don't know. Baby, I'm sorry." I cried.

"Guess."

"Corn, please don't make me answer that."

"How many times, Sasha?"

I inhaled and exhaled a deep breath. "About once every two weeks for a year. Corn, I'm sorry."

"NO! One time is *sorry*, twenty plus times is *I'm a hoe!*" Corn yelled.

Did this man just call me a hoe?

"Tell me this; when was the first time?" He asked glaring at me.

"When we were in Orlando." Corn looked at me like he wanted to kill me. I wouldn't have blamed him if he had.

"I knew those panties that Rae found in the truck were yours but my heart didn't want to believe it. My heart just wouldn't let me believe that my wife, who claims she loves me more than anything, would ever hurt me like that. I kept telling myself that I was wrong and I was just being paranoid or insecure even. How could you do this to me? Why did you do this to me? I don't understand what I did to deserve this. Tell me what I did." He said as a tear ran down his face.

"Corn, you didn't do anything. I was a fool. I don't know why I did it. I'm so sorry. Please don't leave me. Please, Corn...I need you." I said getting down on my knees.

"Did you still need me when you were climbing off of my best friend's dick?" He asked sarcastically.

"Corn, please...."

Corn started giggling. At this point I became very frightened.

"Why are you laughing, Corn?" I asked.

"Because I'm such a damn fool for ever believing anything that ever came out of your damn mouth!" He yelled.

"I didn't mean to hurt you, Corn. Things just got so deep that I didn't know how to get out."

"So, that night I came home from my business trip and found what looked like a passion mark on the back of your neck was from Sylus, huh?" He asked.

I had completely forgotten about that. Everything that I tried to keep from Corn is now coming out and there was no point in lying about it at this point.

"Yes. Sylus had just left about fifteen minutes before you walked in that night." I said looking down at the floor.

Corn jumped up off the bed and threw a punch at the wall knocking a large hole in it.

"Baby, I'm so sorry. Please calm down. I don't know what to say to make you believe me but I really didn't mean for any of this to happen. Please don't leave me." I said still down on my knees.

"You should have thought about that before you dogged me." He said walking out the front door not even looking back at me once.

I collapsed onto the floor and cried myself to sleep.

Chapter Eleven

"Back in the arms of God"

It's been a long four weeks since Cornelius walked out the door. He still hasn't come back. I think he's left me for good. It's been hell since he left. I tried to be strong and keep my head up but I just couldn't. I haven't left my house for three weeks. I can't eat. I can't sleep. I can't think. I can't breathe. Today felt a lot different from the other days. Today, I began to feel like I couldn't live without Corn. A voice in my head was telling me that death would relieve the pain. The voice told me that death was the only way out.

I was feeling so depressed and so down that I figured it would be a good time to go to church. I had such an experience the last time I went to House of Praise so I figured I'd go again. And who knows, maybe I'll see Corn there. I doubt it though. Lately, it feels like he's been erased off the face of the earth. I called his job and they told me he no longer works there. I called his family and they tell me that they haven't seen him since the party. I keep hoping that maybe he just needs some breathing room. Everyday I sit and wait by the front door longing for his return.

I went over to the closet and pulled out this royal purple business suit that I've never worn. It was a pants suit with gold buttons. I put the outfit on and I looked like a million bucks but I still felt like crap. I grabbed my purple purse off the top shelf in my closet, snatched my keys off the counter and headed for the door.

I showed up at the House of Praise right before it was time for Pastor Harvey to preach. He still looked just as handsome as he did the last time I saw him. When I walked into the sanctuary Pastor Harvey planted his eyes right on me. I assumed he remembered me from the last time I was here. Today his sermon came out of II Corinthians 5:17. The bible says that once you have accepted God that you are made new. You are turned into a new creature.

When it came time for invitation to discipleship I felt a familiar heaviness tugging at my chest. *Is this you again, God?* My foot began shaking uncontrollably, my left eyebrow began to twitch and my lips started to quiver.

"There's a lost soul in this place today. God wants you to come home, Beloved. Come to Jesus, my child!" Pastor Harvey yelled in the microphone.

I don't know what got into me. The second he said "Come to Jesus" I was out of my seat and headed to the altar. I cried the whole way there. Pastor Harvey met me at the front of the church. He cried and screamed and cried and for the life of me I couldn't figure out why he was so happy. Once he finished, he grabbed my hands and asked me why I had come to the altar. I told him that I felt alone in this world and I had nothing to live for. I also told him that I was ready to surrender everything over to Jesus. I had nothing more to lose but everything to gain. I told him that I wanted to give my life back to God.

"Why?" He asked.

"Because I've let Satan make a fool of me for far too long. I want to change my life. I want to go to Heaven. I want to come back home, Pastor." I said with boldness that I didn't even know that I had. I was so proud of myself. The pastor lifted his hand up to the sky and began praying over me. As he prayed, my entire life flashed before my eyes. I thought about being raped time and time again, I thought about my mother's suicide, my grandmother's colon cancer, my daddy's beatings and abandonment, my affair with Sylus, my estranged marriage to Corn, the betrayal of my best friend and finally I thought about what my life is going to be after I have made this drastic change in my life. I couldn't wait to feel this promised peace that God has for me. All I wanted was to be back in God's arms again. The more and more I thought about this, the more and more happy I became. Before I knew it I had let out a huge pain filled scream and fell to my knees. With that scream I felt like I had released all the pain, hurt, guilt and perverse demons that had been dwelling within me for all these years. It felt so good to just let it out. It felt so good that I had to scream again and again and again. I cried and cried and cried right there on the soft red carpet right at Pastor Harvey's feet. I was so happy because for the first time, I knew what joy felt like.

Pastor Harvey finally picked me up off the floor and hugged me close to his strong broad chest. I felt like a whole new woman. I knew that from that point on, my life had a purpose and now I have a reason to live. How could I have been mad at God for all those years when all he was trying to do was love me? He had to break me in order to save me. I felt an array of spirit filled chills all over my body. I couldn't stop smiling. I was so happy and excited. I was so happy that I began dancing. Not the normal dancing that I did when I hit the clubs. This dance was different. This was a victory dance. I took fifteen victory laps around the church. Those laps symbolized every trial I had to face, every person that ever hurt me, every mistake that I have ever made, every person that I have hurt in my lifetime, every member of my family that had turned their backs on me, all the times that I was raped and molested, all the times that I was beaten, and finally, it symbolized every demon that tried to break me. The devil thought he had me. But the devil is a liar.

At the end of my victory laps I went over and hugged Pastor Harvey one more time and rested my head on his chest.

"Thank you, Pastor Harvey."

"I knew you would see the light and come back home." He said wiping tears from his cheeks.

Once the service was over I hopped in my car and drove off like a maniac. I was so excited about what had happened at church that I just had to tell someone. I drove home, jumped out the car and flew in through the front door of my red brick two story home. I immediately ran to the phone and began dialing numbers. I was calling my Aunt Lyla.

"Aunt Lyla?" I asked.

"Hey Sweetie! It's so nice to hear your voice. I haven't heard from you in almost a year. How have you been, Honey?" She said with a hearty southern accent.

"It's nice to hear yours too. Aunt Lyla I have to tell you what an amazing Sunday I had!" I yelled in excitement.

"Okay, I'm listening." She said clearing her throat.

"I got saved today! It felt so good and I feel so free. I'm just filled with so much peace and love, Aunt Lyla. I felt the Holy Spirit for the first time on today and I can't wait to feel it again. I feel like my cup is running over. I can't even explain it." I said pacing around in a circle with this non-erasable smile on my face.

"Wow, Sasha! I am so proud of you. You know I found God too. Not too long after I was diagnosed with breast cancer and I prayed and prayed for you. I know you thought nobody cared about you but I did. I love you like you're my own child. You *ARE* my child. That was the best gift that your mother could have ever given me. I know I didn't take care of you like I should have but just know that my heart was in the right place. Despite what you may find out about me later, know that I truly love you." She said with a cry ball in her throat.

Aunt Lyla and I talked for at least two hours about how wonderful God is and how He's changed our lives. That's the longest that I had ever spoken to my aunt. We finally agreed to continue our conversation another day. As I hung the phone up I was startled by a quick shadow that whipped past the corner of my eye.

"Who's there?" I yelled slowly heading to the kitchen to find a knife.

"It's me, Sasha." Corn said walking around the corner right in front of me.

"Corn you scared the heck out of me!" I said grabbing my chest.

"I'm sorry. I just came to pick up my things." He said walking past me.

I grabbed his arm and pulled him closer to me.

"Corn, can we talk?" I asked with a sincere look on my face.

He stared at me for a few moments before finally answering.

"Okay." He said with a frown on his face.

We sat down on our fluffy cream couch.

"Corn, I am so sorry that I hurt you. You know I love you more than anything. I honestly don't know what got into me. I don't want to lose you, Corn." I said holding his hand.

"I heard you on the phone." He responded. I was a little thrown off by his subject change.

"Tell me about it." He said.

"What?" I thought to myself.

"Um…okay. Well it was like a feeling that I have never felt before in my life. I feel so…I can't explain it. It felt like fire shut up in my bones, as the old church folks used to say. It feels good. I feel safe. You know what I mean?" I said with a smile on my face.

"Yeah, I know what you mean. I remember how excited I was when I first found God. What made you want to get up and go to church today?" He asked staring down at his feet.

"Honestly, I felt like it was my only way out. If I had gone to church today and felt no difference…then I was going to come home and slit my wrists. I had nothing to live for. I lost my mom, my dad, my grandmother, my best friend, my husband and most of all I lost myself. What was left?" I said wiping a happy tear from my eye. To my surprise, Corn reached over and put his arms around me.

"I'm happy for you." He whispered in my ear and let go of me.

"Sasha, I want to work things out with you but I don't think I can. I don't think I'm strong enough. I never thought in a million years that you would ever do something like that to me. I could probably forgive you if it happened once or even twice but you did it over and over again for a year. How am I supposed to bear knowing that you made love to another man the same way that you made love to me every night? How am I supposed to go on knowing that he touched you in the very same places that I did? How can a person get over something like that? You were the one person that was always supposed to have my back and be in my corner. How could you betray my trust like that? Do you know how much I love you?"

"I know you love me. I love you too. I've never loved anybody the way that I love you. I don't know why I did it. It was like everything had spun out of control and I was in so deep that I couldn't get out. I don't expect you to just forgive me and go on like nothing happened. I'm just asking you to give me another chance. I'm a new person today. I'm not the same Sasha that I was yesterday. Please give me another chance. You don't even have to live here or anything like that. I just don't want to lose your friendship. I just want you to give me the opportunity to make it up to you. Baby please, I'm so sorry. You have no idea how this has made me feel lower than dirt. Please just give me a chance." I said getting down on my hands and knees with no shame.

Corn placed his elbows on his knees and buried his face in the palms of his hands.

"How do we start over, Sasha? We've been together for twelve years. How do you expect me to erase twelve years of us and start over? How can I do that? Every time I look at you I will be reminded of what you did. I don't think I can do that." He said lifting up his head.

"I don't know. Prayer." I said lifting my eyebrow.

"I have one question, Sasha. Would you have still been sleeping with him had you not gotten caught?" He asked staring me in the eye.

"No. That day that you left him alone with me the day that I had come home from the hospital, I told him that I couldn't do it anymore. In fact, I told him several times that I didn't want to do it anymore. But that last time, I meant it and he knew it. He just wouldn't accept the fact that I wanted to end it so he took it." I said in one big breath.

"What do you mean, *he took it*?" He asked standing to his feet.

"He took it, Corn. Why did you think I didn't want to sleep in our bed that night? Why did you think that I was sitting in the shower about to drown myself? Why did you think I didn't want you to touch me? I felt so violated and ashamed, Corn." I said standing up next to him.

"He raped you?"

I stared down at the floor and did everything I could to avoid eye contact.

"Sasha, look at me. Did he rape you?" He asked picking my face up.

I swallowed hard and finally answered. "Yes."

"In the bed that we slept in?"

"Yes."

Corn just stood there looking into space like a zombie. I guess he didn't really know what to think. He probably thought I deserved it for playing with fire.

"Sasha, why didn't you tell me?"

"How, Corn?"

"Baby, I sat at the table and ate with this man two hours after he raped you? I feel like a damn fool!" He yelled

"Corn…."

"I went and played basketball every Saturday with that dude. I trusted that man in my house while I was gone! He looked at me in my face everyday and acted like everything was great knowing he had been fucking my wife on a daily basis! Damn it, Sasha! How could y'all do this to me?" Corn cried out.

With every tear that fell from his face, I felt more and more guilty and ashamed.

"I don't know what to tell you, Babe. Corn, I'm so sorry." I whimpered.

"You expect me to take you back just because you're sorry? You're damn right *you're sorry!*" He yelled.

"Corn, what can I do to make this up to you?" I asked grabbing his hands.

"At this point…..you can go to hell." He snapped snatching his hands away from mine.

I fell to the floor and cried uncontrollably.

"I can't do this right now, Sasha. I gotta go because if I stay here any longer, I'm afraid I might hurt you." He said walking out the front door and letting it slam behind him.

I didn't know what to think or do. As I sat back on the sofa, the room fell dead silent. I kneeled down on my knees and began to pray.

"Father, I know I've done wrong and I know I don't deserve a man like Cornelius. But God, I love him and I want him back. Please

Lord; touch his heart so that he can find a place in his heart to forgive me. Even if he doesn't come back to me, I pray that you'll help him love again and bless him with a woman that will treat him the way that he deserves to be treated. And Lord, I pray that you'll forgive me too. I love you, Lord and I thank you for loving me even in all my mess. Amen."

Chapter Twelve

"Divorce?"

Several weeks had passed and I still hadn't seen or heard from Corn. I did everything I could to keep my mind off of him but nothing worked. I tried to pick up hobbies such as sewing, tennis and even bowling. I was just too depressed and contaminated by my broken heart. I miss him so much. I miss the way he smelled, the way he smiled, the way he laughed and I even miss the smell of his warm farts at night. My thoughts were interrupted by a loud knock on the door. I walked over to answer it and to my pleasant surprise it was Corn.

"Hey." I said bringing a smile to my face.

"Hey. Can I come in?" He asked sticking is hands in his pockets.

Corn never looked sexier than he did right then. He had on those denim jeans that accentuate his behind in all the right places and a snuggly fit black collared polo shirt that hugged his muscular arms just right. I wanted to eat him up with a giant wooden spoon.

"Of course, it's your house." I said with a giggle.

Corn smiled at that, came into the house and sat on a barstool sitting near the kitchen.

"So what brings you by?" I asked almost confident that he was here to forgive me.

"I've been doing some thinking and I know you're sorry for what you did…but I don't think I can bear being with you or even around you for that matter."

I felt like my heart had just fallen out of my body and hit the cold marble floor.

"Corn, please…" I pleaded beginning to cry.

"Sasha, I don't want to hurt you but I can't do this. I love you, Baby, but I can't." He said standing to his feet.

"Corn, don't say it….please."

"I want a divorce, Baby." He said biting his top lip.

I fell to my knees and cried. I grabbed Corn by the ankles and began begging him not to leave me.

"Sasha, don't do this. Be a woman and have some dignity. Get up off the floor." Corn said picking me up off the floor.

"Corn, what am I supposed to do without you? Please don't leave me." I continued to beg.

Corn stepped closer to me and grabbed my face by my chin. "You should have thought about that before you starting screwing my best friend." He said handing me a folder with divorce papers inside.

"No! I won't do it!" I yelled.

"I don't need your signature to follow through with the divorce but if you just go ahead and sign the papers, it will make things a lot easier. Don't make this more difficult than it has to be. Just sign the damn papers and get it over with. You can keep the car and the house." He said handing me a pen.

I snatched the papers out of Corn's hand, ripped them up and threw them down the garbage disposal. Corn became so angry that I could almost see steam coming out of his ears.

"Damn it, Sasha! Why are you making this complicated?" He yelled.

"Because I love you and there's no way you're going to get rid of me that easy. I won't let you leave me, Corn. I know you still love me."

"Yes, I do still love you, but I cannot be with you. I don't trust you."

"Please…." I pleaded once again. I pulled Corn closer to me and began placing slow sensual kisses on his neck.

"Sasha, stop it." He demanded in a low voice.

I continued kissing him slowly on the neck. The goose bumps forming on his forearms gave me authorization to go further. I slowly began kissing him on the lips. I kissed him with everything I had in me. I needed him to know and to feel how much I truly loved him and how sorry I was. Corn wrapped his arms around me and caressed my back.

"*Yes yes yes!"* I thought to myself.

Corn abruptly removed his hands from my back and brought them up to my face.

"Baby, I can't do this." He struggled to say in between kisses.

"Yes, you can." I smiled at him.

"No, I…I….can't." He yelled pushing my face away from his.

"Corn…."

"I will be back next week with a new set of papers. I have to go." He said trying to walk out the door.

I grabbed him by the shirt and pleaded for him to stay but he wasn't having it. He slapped my grip from his shirt and walked out the door. I was devastated. I cried for three straight days. I felt like I was about to die. If only I had realized how much I truly loved and needed Corn before this whole mess ever occurred, none of this would have ever gone down. I had no one to turn to. I've only had one true friend my entire life and that was Requelle. She'd probably curse me out if I dare called her.

At this point, I do realize that I have one person to turn to, *The Lord.* God is going to have to take complete control of this one because I've done all I can do.

Chapter Thirteen

"Unexpected Surprises"

The past three months have been hell. I'm still just as devastated as I was the very day Corn left. I don't know if I'll ever get over my first love, my confidant, *my soul mate.* I can't help but sit around and comfort myself with memories of the good times Corn and I shared. I believe those memories are the only things keeping me sane right now. There's one memory that stands out more than the rest. My heart smiles just thinking about it.

Thanksgiving Day
1999

Today is Thanksgiving; my least favorite holiday. I hate Thanksgiving. It's supposed to be a time that everybody gets together to celebrate what they're thankful for but I'm not thankful for anything. I hate my life. The only thing good that's happened to me lately is I met my first love, Cornelius Deandre Ross. He's perfect. He is everything that I ever wanted in a man. He's sweet, genuine and so handsome. And he's so smart. I just can't get over how I was able to find such a good man.

He's picking me up in just a minute. We're going to the movies to see Baby Boy. I'll watch anything with Tyrese in it. I'm a huge Tyrese fan.

A metallic black 1999 Honda Accord pulled right in front of my apartment. "I wonder who that is." I said to myself stepping down off the front porch. The driver's door flung open and out came the sexiest man on earth.

"Hey You. You ready to go?" Corn asked leaning up against the driver's side of the car.

I couldn't believe my eyes. "Yeah." I yelled running up and giving him a bear hug.

"You like my new ride?" He asked walking around and opening up the car door for me.

"This ride is dope! When did you get this and how did you get this?" I asked sitting down in my seat and strapping on my seat belt. The inside of the car was just as fly as the outside. It had cream leather seats, a wood grain dash and a six disc CD changer. Corn works full time at House of Tacos down the street but even if he sold a million tacos he wouldn't be able to buy such a nice car.

"You know how I do. I only paid eleven hundred dollars for it. Can you believe that?"

"Eleven hundred dollars? Why would someone sell this car so cheap?" I was very curious to see what he was going to say.

"Let's just say, they needed the money real bad and in a hurry. So he sold it to me. I kind of feel bad because I know this car is worth much more. But hey, that's life."

"Yeah, I guess. What movie theater are we going to?" I asked looking over at him.

"Um…actually I was hoping we could go somewhere else." He said twisting up the side of his face.

"Somewhere else?" I asked lifting my eyebrows at him.

"Somewhere we can talk and stuff. Today *is* our four year anniversary. I really wanted to take this thing to the next level." He said cheesing at me.

My lip began quivering out of sheer fear. I love Corn to death and I would love to take this thing to the next level but the last person I had sex with was Pastor Mayvis and it was terrible. And it hurt like hell. I felt nervousness in the pit of my stomach. I felt like I was about to throw up and then my throw up was going to throw up. I sat there fiddling with my fingernails the whole way to the hotel.

We pulled up to the Royal Island hotel. I waited in the car while Corn went in to get the keys. I was seriously thinking about just jumping out the car and running for the border. Right as I was about to unlock my door, I saw Corn walking back to the car.

"I didn't take too long, did I?" He giggled getting back into the car and shutting the door.

We drove around the corner to the back side of the hotel. We walked up two flights of stairs and we finally arrived at our room. We were in room two nineteen. Before we walked in, Corn covered my eyes with a yellow bandana. He led me in through the door and sat me down on the soft bed. I could smell fresh flowers all around me. I felt like I was back in my back yard when I was a little girl sitting in my mom's flower bed. She had all kinds of flowers and plants; daisies, tulips, elephant ears, sunflowers, gladiolas and she even had some aloe vera plants. She used to put the clear ooze from the leaves of the aloe vera in my hair to make it grow. I guess it worked too because my hair is half way down my back.

Corn untied the bandana and pulled it off my eyes. I stood to my feet, flung my mouth open and then covered it with my hand.

"Do you like it?" Corn asked with a proud smile on his face.

There were red, pink and white rose pedals everywhere. They were on the bed, the dresser, the floor, the sitting table, the TV and even in the bathroom. He had taken the dingy hotel spread off the bed and replaced it with a fluffy pink silky comforter with several pink, red and white pillows of all different sizes and shapes. He had candles lit everywhere, at least fifty. I was flabbergasted. The cat really had my tongue. I tried to speak but nothing would come out at first. Everything was so beautiful.

"I love it. How did you do all of this? This is so nice. No one has ever done anything this nice for me. Thank you so much. You have really made my day. I love you so much." I said walking over to him and crying on his shoulder.

"Baby, don't cry. You know your man will do anything to see that beautiful smile on your face. I love you, Sasha." He said lifting my head up.

He then reached into his pocket and pulled out a little blue box.

"What's that?" I asked.

"Open it and see."

I opened the little blue box and inside was a beautiful diamond sitting on top of a silver band. It was the most beautiful engagement ring that I had ever seen.

"Corn….." I said covering my mouth.

He pulled the ring out of the box and slid it on my trembling finger. "Sasha, will you marry me?"

"Yes." I said on the verge of tears.

I stared him in his eyes and I immediately felt a spark shoot all the way up my spine. I was so aroused and amazed at how beautiful this man was that I just couldn't contain it. I grabbed his face with both of my hands and practically in gulped him. He was very shocked by this but he went with the flow. I laid on the fluffy bed, pulled him by the front of his shirt and pulled him down on top of me. I parted my legs and allowed him to lie in between. He unbuttoned my top and peeled it off of my fully aroused body. He massaged my breast with his lips. I had never felt like this before. He then worked his way down to the lower part of my body and lifted up my skirt. First he kissed my outer thighs and then my inner thighs then worked his way between my legs. Next thing I knew, I heard a sucking slurping sound and felt a feeling that I had never felt before. Whatever he was doing down there was making my body move and wiggle like I had ants in my pants. For the first time, I knew what pleasure felt like. Ten minutes later he came back up for air and began kissing my neck. He lifted one of my legs up in the air and slid himself in. It felt like a place that I had never been before but only heard about. After about twenty minutes, I tried to speak but all I could do was scream. My screams grew closer and closer to each other like contractions until it became one big scream and the beast that I had lying inside of me had been released. All of my energy had been drained out from head to toe. When Corn finally pulled out I felt so at ease and calm. It was the best experience of my life. I felt like I had released every thing that had ever held me down in life. All my anger, pain, frustrations and anxieties had been replaced with the love that I have for this man. And most importantly, I finally got the chance to experience love in its physical form.

"Are you okay?" Corn asked completely out of breath.

"I'm great. That was the best feeling I had ever felt in my life. I really needed that." I said looking over at him and smiling.

Corn started laughing. "Yeah, I had to put it on ya! You might as well give up now, I got you sprung!"

Corn and I laughed and played for the remainder of the evening, went to sleep and did the same thing over again the next day. *And the day after that.*

I had been having terrible stomach pain for about two months. I went to my doctor, Dr. Barnes. He's been my doctor for almost ten years. When I told him about my stomach pain and morning dizziness he suggested that I take a pregnancy test. I thought he was crazy. "There's no way I'm pregnant!" I thought to myself. Dr. Barnes was the one that told me that I was unable to have children do to the damage that was done by Pastor Mayvis which is also why I don't have a monthly cycle.

I went ahead and took the test anyway just to humor him and to my surprise, the dang thing came up positive! I was four months pregnant.

No, there's no way!

"NO, NO, NO! Dr. Barnes, I can't be pregnant!" I yelled jumping off the paper covered table and almost ripping my paper dress.

"Sorry, Ms. Ross but you are." He said showing me the pregnancy results for the fifth time.

"What am I going to do? Dr. Barnes, I had an affair that ended four months ago. If I had sex with one man fifty times and the other one a hundred times, would there be a better chance that the man I did it a hundred times with is the father?" I said with a hopeful frown.

"No, Sasha. It's a *fifty fifty* chance no matter how many times you had sex with one or the other if you slept with them around the same time." He said giggling at me.

Please, God! This can't be Sylus' baby.

I ran home and prayed like I never prayed before. Although, I know that no sin goes unpunished. "But God, Please have mercy!" I cried out loud. I was so upset. I needed someone to talk to so, of all people, I picked up the phone and called my best friend that I hadn't spoken to in four months.

I picked up my pink razor phone and began dialing Requelle's number. I've been trying to talk to Rae for the past three months but she refused to talk to me. I know I've probably called her a million times. I'll keep trying until she agrees to talk to me.

"Hello?" Rae answered in a very worn out voice. I was so surprised that she even answered the phone.

"Hey Rae. Will you please talk to me?" I asked.

"I answered the phone, didn't I?" She snapped.

"Okay. You want to talk over the phone or would you like to meet somewhere." I asked hoping she would agree to meet me. I really wanted to see her.

"I'll meet you at the Whataburger on Main." She said hanging up without even warning me first.

I got over to the restaurant about eleven minutes later. I looked around and finally found Rae sitting at a lonely booth. She looked horrible. Her hair looked like it hadn't been combed in days. She had on a pair of baggy grey sweatpants and a plain white t-shirt. As I began walking over towards her I felt a lump of regret and worry in my throat. I finally made it to her and sat down on the opposite side of the booth she was sitting in.

"Hey." I said staring at her and biting my lip. Rae didn't even respond. She just sat there looking at me like, *"Let's get this shit over with."* And I did just that.

"Rae, I can't express to you how sorry I am for hurting you. There are no words. I wanted to tell you. I just didn't know…"

"You wanted to tell me? When; after the first time, fifth time or maybe the tenth time?" She yelled interrupting me mid sentence.

"I'm sorry, Rae."

"Is that all you wanted to say to me? You could have told me *that shit* over the phone." She said folding her arms in front of her chest.

"What do you want me to say?" I asked throwing my arms up.

"Tell me why you have made my life a living hell! Tell me why the only person in the world that I truly called a friend has betrayed me with the only man that I've ever loved! Tell me why you chose to mess with my husband out of all the things that you could've done to hurt me! Tell me!" She yelled.

"*RAE!* I don't know! I don't know why I did it. I never set in my heart to hurt you. You are the last person I wanted to hurt. It just happened! I feel terrible about the whole thing. I'm sorry! That's all I can say. There's nothing that I can do that will make this go away. You can either forgive me or hate me but either way I'm moving past this with baby and all!" I cried.

Rae just stared at me with no response. She brought her hand up to her mouth as tears began to run down her chocolate cheeks.

"What? What did I say?" I asked in a state of confusion.

"You're pregnant?" She asked lowering her boney hand.

Oops, Did I say that?

"Yes… But don't jump to conclusions. This could be Corn's baby. In fact, I'm pretty sure this is Corn's baby." I said putting my hand over hers.

"No, this is Sylus' baby. I know it is because that's the kind of luck I have. I can't believe this. What am I going to do, Sasha?"

I had no idea why she was asking *me* that. I scooted over to her side of the booth and wrapped my arms around her. She looked over at me with a teary eyed face, got up from the booth and walked away. I had no idea what was going through her head just then but I knew it wasn't good. Rae has never been very stable. She's always reacted to things a whole lot different from most people. I was scared and didn't know what to think.

I pray Rae doesn't do anything to make things worse.

Chapter Fourteen

"Love is powerful"

      It's been five months since my conversation with Rea. I guess all of this was just too much for her to take. Neither Sylus nor Rae have called or even spoken to me. If Sylus loved me the way he said he did, you would think that he would have at least called. *Bastard!* I've had to go through this pregnancy all by myself. This has been a very rough pregnancy. I'm in and out of hospitals every other week because of high blood pressure, low iron in my blood, over exhaustion and stress. I'm due any day now. I can't wait to meet my baby. This baby is all I have right now so I'm going to hold on to him tight and never let go. I'm going to name him Cornelius Deandre Ross II whether Corn's the father or not. I'll call him CJ for short. I love CJ more than anything in this world. He's the only person that I can honestly say I would die for.

      A lot has happened since Corn left me. Word around town is he has a new girlfriend. Supposedly, her name is Lisa. I hear she's very beautiful and sophisticated. I'm not sure how serious things are but for my sake I hope she's just his rebound girl. I still think about

Corn everyday but I'm finally coming around. I've finally realized that I have to move on. I have to be strong for CJ. If I can't stay sane for myself, I can at least do it for my baby. I've thought about calling Corn and Sylus and letting them know about the baby. But I quickly decided not to. It would just cause more drama.

I walked outside to pick up my Sunday morning paper and heard splattering against the pavement.

Oh my God, my water just broke!

I immediately walked into the house and into the living room. I picked up the phone and called Pastor Harvey to tell him that I wouldn't be at church today. He was so happy to hear that the baby was coming. He said the church would be praying for me and he hung up. I then called my doctor and told him I was going into labor. He told me to take a cab to the Memorial Hospital and he would meet me there in ten minutes. Dr. Barnes has really helped me throughout this entire pregnancy. He called me once a week to see if I needed anything, he bought a cradle for my baby and tons of diapers and he even signed me up for this single parenting program. I really felt like he cared.

I finally arrived at the Memorial Hospital. Dr. Barnes arrived at the same time I did. He immediately got me a room and had the nurses prep me up. They put me in a bed, put my legs in cold silver plated stirrups and shined a big bright spot light in between my legs. Dr. Barnes couldn't stress enough how important it was that no mistakes were made in delivering CJ. I was a special case because I had an abnormal uterus.

"I can't believe this!" One of the young blonde nurses yelled looking down in between my legs.

"What is it?" I said grabbing my chest out of pure fright.

"How long have you been in labor?" The nurse asked.

"I don't know, maybe about two hours or so. What's wrong? Is my baby okay?"

"He's ready to come out! I can see the top of his head peeking. I didn't expect him to come so soon. Don't worry though. You'll be fine and so will this baby." She said putting on these long plastic gloves and a plastic face guard.

"But I haven't had my epidural yet!" I yelled frantically.

Then came the pain. I thought I was dying. I had never felt a pain like that in my entire life. My body trembled and ached.

"Okay Sasha, it's time to push. You're going to give me a big ten second push, ok? You can do this. I know it hurts." Dr. Barnes said covered in gloves, face masks and scrubs.

I took a deep painful breath and pushed with all my might.

"Okay, I can see his head peeking. Give me one more push! You can do this."

I took another breath and pushed again. At the end of the push all the pain I was enduring had ceased. Then I heard the sweet sound of a faint baby cry. It was like music to my ears. The nurses took the baby, cut the umbilical cord, put him in a plastic tray and washed him off. They then handed him back to Dr. Barnes.

"Here is your beautiful healthy baby boy." He said handing him to me. The nurses wrapped me in a warm sheet but I was still freezing. I was shivering uncontrollably. Dr. Barnes told me that this was normal. My body was in shock. It stopped after a couple of hours.

My baby was so beautiful. He had the biggest dark brown eyes and the softest fair skinned face. He had a head full of thick curly black hair. He looked just like his mama. He was so perfect. I held him in my arms until we both went to sleep. The nurses came a little later that evening and took him to the nursery. I was so thankful to God that we both made it. I don't know if I could have gone on without CJ. In just one day, he has brought so much joy to my life. He was truly a gift from God.

The next morning I woke up feeling totally rejuvenated. I couldn't wait to see my baby. As I started climbing out of the tall bed I saw the back of a tall muscular man staring out the window.

"Can I help you?" I asked.

The tall man turned and stared right into my eyes. I was shocked and confused when I realized who it was.

"Hey Sash." Julius said walking towards me.

Julius is Corn's older brother. We call him *Ju Ju*. He's just as fine as Corn and always has been. He's tall, fine as hell and has the prettiest hazel eyes I've ever seen on a man.

"Ju Ju, what are you doing here? How did you even know that I was here?" I asked in a very concerned voice.

"I actually didn't know that you were here. My mom developed a heart condition and I brought her into the hospital yesterday afternoon because she's been having chest pain and I saw you being wheeled in. This was purely a coincidence." He smiled at me. He had a smile just like Corn's.

"I see. Well, how have you been, Ju?"

"I've been pretty good. I see you're doing pretty well too, huh?" He chuckled.

I giggled at that.

"So who's the lucky man?" He asked.

I didn't know what to tell him so I lied. "Oh, you wouldn't know him. He's not from here."

"Why isn't he here with you?"

"We're not together anymore. He doesn't want anything to do with this child. I'm going to raise him by myself." I said with a straight face.

"That's going to be pretty rough on you, don't you think?" He asked raising his eyebrows.

"Ju Ju, can we please just drop this?" I said becoming very irritated.

"Sure we can. I didn't mean to get all up in your business. I'm just a little worried about you." He said sitting down on the hospital bed.

"Well, thank you for caring."

"Sasha, I really want to talk to you about Corn." He said changing the tone in his voice.

"What about?"

"Sash, I don't know if you know this but Corn is about to get married. And I think he's making a big mistake."

"Married?....Are you serious?" I asked in disappointment.

"Yes. I mean, you guys haven't even been divorced a year yet and he's already getting married. There's something not right about that. He's not ready for this." Ju Ju said talking with his hands.

"Julius, Corn hasn't spoken to me since we finalized the divorce. Whatever he has going on in his life has nothing to do with me."

"Yes it does, Sash. I know he's still in love with you. I know he'll never be truly happy unless he's with you. You're his soul mate. He's just upset right now and he's hurt."

"What are you asking me to do?"

"Just call him and talk this thing out with him. Tell him he's making a mistake. I've tried to tell him but he won't listen to me." He said standing to his feet.

"I'm sorry, Ju Ju, but I can't. Corn made it clear to me that he wants nothing to do with me so I have to respect that."

Ju Ju inhaled a deep breath and let out a big sigh. "I understand. Here's his card just in case you change your mind." He said handing me Corn's business card and walking away.

I didn't know what to make of that conversation. I can't believe that Corn is already engaged and we just got officially divorced six months ago. She must be *some* woman. All this time I've been waiting for Corn to come running back to me. After having this conversation I know that won't be happening any time soon. Of course I can't say that I don't deserve it.

It was finally time for CJ and me to go home. I was so happy but at the same time I had no idea how to take care of a baby. He was so tiny. I didn't want to accidentally hurt him. He was only five pounds and seven ounces. Every time he cried, I wanted to run him back to the hospital just in case something was wrong. When I was dressing him to go home from the hospital, I accidentally snapped his skin in one of the snaps of his little jumpsuit. I felt terrible. CJ cried and cried for twenty minutes. The nurse told me it was okay but I still felt like a horrible mother. Once I got the baby home, he started crying so I assumed he was hungry. I fed him until he didn't want anymore. Then he coughed and a bunch of white stuff came out of his mouth. It scared the hell out of me. I ran to the phone and called the nurse again. She laughed. "Its okay, Mrs. Kirk. You probably overfed him. Don't worry you'll get the hang of it." She said. I felt like an idiot. *Lord, help me.*

With Corn's very comfortable alimony payments, I finally built up enough courage to quit my job. I wanted to spend all the time I could with CJ. I want him to have everything that I didn't growing up. I never had parents that were there for me. My parents never attended my PTA meetings or teacher parent conferences. I didn't have parents that took me to the park to play or Chuck E. Cheese's for my birthdays. My parents weren't there. I'm going to do my best to give my baby the world at all costs.

Chapter Fifteen

"God Works in Mysterious Ways"

CJ is now six weeks old. He's gotten so big. I still can't tell who he looks like. Some days he's looks identical to Sylus and other days his facial expressions remind me of Corn. The fact that Corn is getting married just hit me about a week ago. It hit me hard. I almost broke down but the smiles on CJ's face kept me going. Corn's wedding day is in three days. I decided that I'd rather not hang around for that. CJ and I are going to Jamaica to get some sun, relax and allow things to die down. I believe there comes a time in everybody's life when you have to escape from your surroundings and travel to some place new and different. Now is that time for me.

The phone began to ring as I was placing diapers in my suitcase. I didn't really feel like talking to anyone so I allowed the answering machine to pick it up.

"This is Sasha. Leave a message at the beep."

"Hey Sash, this is Corn. I was calling because I really needed to talk….."

My heart almost skipped a beat at the mere sound of Corn's voice. I reached over and grabbed the phone before he could even finish his sentence.

"Hey, I'm here." I said in a pant trying not to seem too enthused that he was calling me.

"Hey. Um…can I come over so we can talk?" He asked with a shaky voice.

"Sure you can. What time?"

"I'm outside."

I immediately ran to the bathroom, fingered through my hair and smeared on some cherry red lipstick. I walked to the front door and turned the doorknob. Corn was standing there in the door way looking good as usual. He had on baggy Phatfarm jeans, a tan and chocolate striped collared shirt and some brown Polo boots. That shirt hugged his chest and arms just right. I did everything I could not to faint.

"Hi." I said fidgeting and looking down at the floor.

"Hey. How are you?" He asked.

The sound of his sexy voice produced perspiration down below.

"I'm okay. Please come in." I said motioning for him to come in.

"Would you like something to drink?" I asked as we plopped down on the sofa.

"Uh…no. I don't plan to be here long."

"Okay."

"I'm not sure if you heard but….I'm getting married this Saturday." He said stroking his goatee.

"Yeah, I heard." I said trying to hold back my disappointment and tears.

"I thought maybe we both needed to clear the air between us. I thought maybe we needed some closure."

"I guess you're right but I really have nothing more to say. I think I've said it all. I told you how sorry I was. I told you that I still love you and I wanted to be with you and you walked out the door. What's left to be said?"

"I guess you're right." He said gazing into my eyes.

"Corn, I……" I was interrupted by CJ's cries.

O crap! I completely forgot about CJ!

I ran to the nursery and picked CJ up out of his crib and brought him out to the living room. I had no idea how I was going to explain this to Corn. I decided not to even try.

Corn looked at the baby and then back at me several times before finally asking, "Whose baby is that?"

"Um….he's a friend of mine's baby." I said as my heart pounded like a hammer on a nail.

"That's funny because he has your eyes." Corn said resting his elbows on his knees.

I began to feel a little uneasy. "I guess that *is* funny."

"Do you have something you want to tell me, Baby?"

"No."

"No, I think you do." He said getting very stern with me.

I took a deep breath. "This is my baby, Corn."

"Who is the father?" He asked getting up out of his seat and folding his arms in front of his chest.

"Corn, I'm really not….."

"I only need a one word answer." He said interrupting me.

"I don't know."

"What do you mean *you don't know*?"

"Corn, I don't know!" I yelled at him standing to my feet.

"What, you don't remember who you've slept with? Has it been that many?"

Before I even knew how to react to what he had just said to me, I had already lifted my hand and slapped him across the face. I slapped him so hard that it left a pink hand print on his yellow cheek. I literally slapped the taste out of his mouth. Corn grabbed me by my chin.

"I've never put my hands on you so do you ever put your hands on me!" He yelled letting go of my face.

"I don't want to fight with you, Corn." I said wiping tears from my face with the back of my hand.

"I don't want to fight with you either."

"Okay. So why don't you just leave then?"

"Not until you answer my question."

I just stood there staring at him like he was crazy hoping that he would get frustrated and leave. But he just stared back. I almost forgot how stubborn he was.

"I only cheated on you with one man our entire relationship. It's either you or him."

"Was that so hard? Why didn't you tell me when you first found out about your pregnancy?"

"Because you were nowhere to be found and plus, I've already decided that I'm going to raise this baby by myself."

"Like Hell!"

"Corn, this isn't up for debate. Look, CJ and I have a plane to catch so…."

"What does CJ stand for?" He asked getting in my face.

I let out a big sigh and walked around him into my bedroom to get my luggage.

"Sasha, I asked you a question." He said following behind me.

"Yeah, I know you did." I said still avoiding the question.

"Well?"

"Can we please talk about this when I come back from Jamaica? I will be back in about a week. Don't you have a wedding to prepare for anyway?" I asked rolling my eyes at him.

Corn didn't say another word and finally left. I didn't know what else to do so I finished packing my bags and left for the airport.

The Day before the Wedding

Corn and about fifteen of his friends and male family members went out to Shiny Poles, a local strip joint, for Corn's bachelor party. Shiny Poles is known for having every man's fantasy.

"Corn, you ready to do this, man?" Ju Ju asked bringing Corn a drink from the bar.

"Man, get that out of here. You know I don't drink." Corn said with a chuckle.

"O yeah, I forgot. You a Christian man, huh?" He said patting him on the knee.

"Yes, I am and don't you ever forget it." He said laughing and taking a sip of his cranberry juice.

"So are you ready?"

"Honestly….I don't know." He answered letting out a big sigh.

"Boy, are you crazy? You are marrying this woman tomorrow and *you don't know*?" He asked looking at Corn crazy.

"Man… I mean, Lisa is beautiful, successful, intelligent, and she has a smile that can light up a room….but I'm just not sure if that's what I really want."

"Please tell me you didn't wait until the day before your wedding to figure that out. I told you the day you asked that woman to marry you that you weren't ready. Why didn't you listen?"

"Man, I don't know. I was cool until I went to see Sasha the other day." Corn said looking down at his fingers.

"What happened with Sasha?" Ju Ju asked waiting to hear something juicy.

"Well, I really just went over there to talk to her and to see how she was doing. Man, she is so beautiful. I couldn't keep my eyes off of her. That woman still makes me weak in the knees even after all the bull she's put me through."

"Sounds like you still love her."

"I do." Corn said with a frown on his face.

"What are you going to do?"

"I don't know. This situation is more complicated now. Did you know Sasha had a baby?"

"Uh…no, I didn't know that." Ju Ju said lying through his teeth.

"Yeah, she doesn't know if the baby is mine or Sylus'. Ain't that messed up? Damn that woman!" He yelled getting angry.

"I told you way back in the day that Sylus wasn't about nothing no way. I knew he wanted what you had. I could tell by the way he looked at her."

"I know but I never thought he would do me like this. He was supposed to be my boy. He smiled in my face by day then screwed my wife by night. I don't understand how he could be so cold. I've never been hurt so bad in my life. And don't even get me started on Sasha. I can't believe her either. Why do I still love her after all of that? Am I a fool?"

"You're not a fool. You can't control who you love. You and Sasha have a lot of history together and a lot of memories. It could take you years to get over her if you ever get over her. You know she didn't purposely set in her heart to hurt you like that."

"I guess." He said getting teary eyed.

"What y'all niggas over here talking about?" Bobby, Corn's younger brother, said stumbling over to where they were sitting.

"Corn's still in love with Sasha." Ju Ju blurted out.

"Ju Ju."

"What? After she dogged you the way she did?"

"She made a mistake." Ju Ju said coming to Sasha's defense.

"Mistake? Yeah right! She's a hoe!" Bobby yelled.

"Bobby, watch your mouth!" Ju Ju yelled back.

"Don't talk about my wife like that!" Corn yelled.

"You mean your *ex*-wife." Bobby added sarcastically.

"Bobby, that's enough." Ju Ju said.

"No, Ju. Look, I love Sasha like a sister but she was wrong for what she did to you, Corn. You didn't deserve that from them. You're going to give up Lisa to be with a woman who obviously doesn't want you?"

"I don't know what I'm going to do. Let's drop it and enjoy the rest of our evening, ok?" Corn said in a calm voice.

The next day Corn sat on the edge of his hotel room bed fully dressed in his creamy white wedding suit.

"God, please tell me what to do. Give me a sign or something." Corn said looking up at the ceiling.

He picked up the remote that was sitting on the edge of the coffee table and turned the television on. The news was on. Corn became horrified as he watched a recording of a commercial plane crash and explode. He watched closely to see where the plane was departing from. He became petrified when it was revealed that the plane was departing from Atlanta and into Jamaica. He remembered Sasha saying that she'd talk to him when she got back from Jamaica and his heart began to race. He could barely breathe he was so frozen with fear.

"Whew! This is the big day, Corn. You ready to jump the broom *again?*" Bobby said with a funny looking smile on his face looking equally attractive in his suit and tie.

Corn completely ignored him and ran and grabbed his phone.

"Corn, what's wrong?"

Corn frantically dialed in Sasha's cell phone number.

"You've reached Sasha. I'm not in right now but please leave me a detailed message at the beep. God bless you. Beeeeeeeeep."

"Sasha, Baby call me as soon as you get this message. I need to hear your voice." He said in a panic.

"Corn, you're scaring me. What is wrong?!" Bobby asked again.

Corn still didn't answer.

He sat back down on the edge of the bed to see if there was anymore information about the plane crash. A list of names scrolled across the screen of people who were on the plane.

"Ju Ju! Something's wrong with Corn!" Bobby shouted.

"What?" Ju Ju asked flying out of the bathroom.

Corn stared a hole in every name that scrolled across the T.V. screen.

"NO NO....please God, don't let this be true." Corn said burying his face in his hands and weeping.

"Corn, what are you talking about? Talk to us. You're scaring us." Ju Ju said picking Corn's head up.

"Sasha and the baby were on the plane that crashed." Corn said barely able to speak.

"What are you talking about?" Bobby asked.

"Look at the T.V."

Bobby and Ju Ju watched in terror. The names scrolled across the screen a second time and there Sasha Ross' name was clear as day. The three of them sat in the room for hours full of regrets and emotions. They were startled by a knock at the door.

Before Bobby could even turn the doorknob to let the person in, Lisa and her entourage of angry bride's maids had already flown through the door.

"Corn! What is going on? We were supposed to be getting married two hours ago! Why did you leave me standing at the altar?" Lisa yelled full of tears.

Lisa was very beautiful. She had shoulder length curly hair with blonde and gold streaks, pretty coco brown skin and big dark brown eyes.

"Lisa, I'm sorry." He said under his breath.

"What's going on?" She asked again.

"Baby, I'm sorry. I can't marry you." Corn said looking up at her with bloodshot teary eyes.

Lisa sat down beside him. "Why? Are you okay?'

"Sasha..."

"O, this has something to do with *Sasha*? I am tired of you constantly talking about your ex-wife! Are you in love with her or me?" She asked sarcastically.

Corn turned and faced her.

"Lisa, I can't marry you because I don't love you. Baby...."

"What do you mean, *you don't love me?*"

"I'm sorry. I can't."

"Why did you ask me to marry you, Corn?"

"Please, just leave. I don't mean to be rude...."

"Did you really just ask me to leave? You're treating me like a nobody? Like a two dollar whore?!" She yelled standing to her feet.

"Don't make this difficult. I don't love you. I'm doing you a favor by not marrying you because the truth of the matter is I would just end up leaving you later. Please just leave."

"No, I won't, Corn!"

"Lisa, *LEAVE!*" Corn yelled so loud that it scared her. She finally gave Corn one last stare and walked out crying so hard that she was barely able to stand. Her bride's maids practically had to carry her out.

"Everybody, please just leave me alone for a minute." Corn said lowering his voice.

"Call us if you need us." Ju Ju said giving Corn a brotherly hug. The second Bobby and Ju Ju left, Corn completely broke down. It took all of this to happen for him to realize how much he truly loved Sasha even though she had hurt him so badly. Corn felt so lost in his sorrow that all he could do was pray and ask God to heal his broken heart.

"God, please help me. I don't know what to do. I need your help, Father. Please fix my heart and help me to love again. In Jesus' name I pray, Amen."

Corn woke up the next morning and decided to return to the home that he and Sasha once shared. He felt that maybe he would get some closure and relief if he went back to the house of memories. He pulled up in front of the house and sat in his car for an hour before he actually went in. He finally built up enough courage to stick his key in the keyhole and turn the doorknob. As he began walking in, he could smell the scent of Sasha's perfume in the air. The scent in the air brought a smile to Corn's face. Corn walked through the kitchen and down the hall to the master bedroom. He sat down on the edge of their king size sleigh bed, rested his elbows on his knees, closed his eyes and tried his hardest not to shed a tear.

"Corn?"

Corn opened his eyes and stood to his feet. "Sasha?" He whispered.

"What are you doing here? Shouldn't you be on your honeymoon or something?" I asked a little bit confused.

Corn grabbed me by my waist and hugged me as tight as he could.

"Boy, what on earth is wrong with you?" I said rubbing his back.

"I thought you were dead."

"Dead?"

"I saw the plane crash on T.V. and you were on the list of people who were on that plane. Baby, I've never been so scared in my life." He said still holding me.

I smiled at that. "I'm fine. God told me not to go so I got off the plane last minute and CJ and I came back home. I'm fine, Corn."

"I forgive you for everything, Baby." He said loosening his hold around my waist.

"What are you saying?"

"The thought of me actually never seeing you again almost killed me. I know I won't love another woman the way that I love you. There's no point in me even trying. I love you, Baby. I know it's going to take a long time for me to fully trust you again but I'm willing to try to make this work if you are."

"Are you serious?" I asked while happy tears filled my eye sockets.

Corn didn't answer me. He grabbed my face and gave me a long sensual kiss in the mouth. It felt so good that I almost had an orgasm. I don't think Corn has ever kissed me like this before. I always loved the way I felt when Corn held me. I feel so safe in his arms. Corn and I broke from our kiss and smiled at each other for a few seconds. Then Corn began to face reality.

"We still need to talk about this baby. Where is he?" Corn asked.

My smile immediately evaporated from my face. "He's sleeping in his crib."

"Is that my baby, Sash?" He asked.

"I told you before; I don't know, Baby. I hope he's yours. I *pray* that he's yours but I really have no idea." I answered looking down at my feet.

"Well, let's go get tested then. I have to know." He said walking to the baby's room.

"Corn….again, I'm….I'm so sorry for all of this."

"Stop apologizing. I know." He said smiling at me.

Corn and I went to a doctor friend of Corn's and got a DNA test done. The doctor said he would let us know the results in a couple of days. All we can do now is wait and hope for the best.

Chapter Sixteen

"Requelle Denise Wyatt"

Lately, I feel like I'm walking on air. Nothing in this world can make me happier than I am at this very moment. Corn and I are doing really well. Things are finally getting back to normal after almost a year and a half. We're finally starting to be the way we used to be and I give God all the glory for that. I understand now that God works in mysterious ways. Everything that happened to me in the past happened for a reason. I guess God definitely used my sins to get my attention. Had all that stuff not happened to me, I probably wouldn't be saved today. God knew exactly what he was doing. God has turned all my negatives into positives. I just hate that it took all hell breaking loose for me to understand.

I haven't heard from Requelle since she found out that I was pregnant. I wish she would return my calls. I left several messages for her to call me back so that we could get in touch. I guess she still wants nothing to do with me. It's just so strange that I haven't seen her around or bumped into her at the grocery store or anything. This really saddens me sometimes. I hate that I lost the only girlfriend that

I had. I wish I could take all the pain she endured but I can't. I wish we were still friends. I miss her so much. I just want to know how she's doing and if she's okay.

I walked into the living room where Corn and the baby were watching a football game. It was the Cowboys and the Giants. I sat down on the sofa and laid my head on his shoulder.

"What's wrong, Baby?" He asked rubbing my cheeks with the back of his hand.

"I miss Requelle. Why won't she call me back? I know what I did was unforgivable but it's been almost two years. You would think that she would at least call or something." I said wiping a tear from my eye. Corn picked up the remote and cut the TV off.

"Sasha, I've been waiting to tell you this because I wanted to make sure that you were ready to hear this. Plus, we've been so happy lately and I didn't want to mess that up." He said turning to me and grabbing my hands.

"What are you talking about?" I asked fearful of what he was about to reveal.

Corn sunk his head down. "Baby, Requelle...Requelle killed herself six months ago." He said lifting his head back up.

"No...no she didn't. She's not dead, she's just doesn't want to see me. No!" I screamed jumping to my feet.

Corn grabbed me and held me close. "Sasha, I'm sorry. I wish I didn't have to tell you this. Just know that this wasn't your fault. She made that choice for herself."

All I could think about was all the good times Requelle and I shared. She was my very best friend and now she's gone. Everything in me wanted to believe that it wasn't true but I knew in my heart that it was. I never even got to say goodbye.

Corn and I sat back down on the couch.

"How did she kill herself? How do you know?" I asked looking up at him with teary eyes.

"I know because I was there."

Requelle's House
March 9, 2007

"Hello?" Corn asked flipping open his cell phone.

"Corn? This is Requelle. I know I haven't spoken to you in a while but you are the only person that I could call." Requelle cried.

"What's going on, Rae? Are you in trouble or something?" Corn asked sitting his bottled water on the counter.

"Sylus and I are fighting and I'm scared. I think he's going to hurt me. Can you please come over?"

"Okay, I'll be there in five minutes. I'm at the gym right up the street from you." Corn said in a panic.

"Okay. Bye." Rae said hanging up.

Corn hopped in his white BMW 745 and drove off. He arrived at Requelle's house three minutes later. He could hear Sylus and Requelle screaming at each other. As he stepped out of his car and began running toward the front door he heard a loud boom shatter the air. He was very familiar with that sound. It was a double barrel shot gun. He knew that sound very well because he used to go hunting with his dad when he was little.

The sound of that shot gun scared the hell out of Corn. He ran and kicked through the front door. He walked in and everything was dead silent. He walked around the corner to the living room and saw Sylus lying on his back covered in blood. Sylus just laid there coughing and spitting up blood and his insides. Corn heard silent whimpers coming from the kitchen. He walked in through the living room and into the kitchen. He then saw Requelle sitting in Indian style in a corner near the glass top stove. Requelle had the shot gun in her hands. She slowly began lifting it up bringing it to her mouth. Corn was horrified. Before he could even say a word, Rae had put the double barrel in her mouth and pulled the trigger. Her brains splattered all over the kitchen walls. The back half of her skull parted from the rest of her body and hit the white tile floor. The rest of her lifeless body finally limped over and died.

Corn ran over to Sylus to see if he was still alive. Sylus continued to spit up blood and chips of his insides. As Corn ran for the phone to call an ambulance he realized that he didn't hear Sylus moving around anymore. Corn sat the phone back on the hook when he realized that Sylus was dead. Corn put both of his hands on his head and fell to the floor. He couldn't believe how this story had ended. Sy and Rae were two of his best friends. He didn't understand why Rae did what she did. He definitely didn't understand why Rae called him to witness it.

Corn finally built up enough strength to call the police. They arrived in less than fifteen minutes. Once they finished questioning him, he got in his car and drove home haunted be the memories of two people that he once called friends.

"Corn, why did you wait so long to tell me?" I asked still in tears.

"Baby, I wasn't sure if you were ready to hear it. Plus, I'm still not over it. I've never seen that much blood in my life. I *still* have nightmares about what I saw that night. You were so happy. I just didn't want to ruin it." He said burying his face in the palms of his hands.

"I'm not mad or anything, I'm just shocked. I can't believe this happened. Why did she do that?"

"I don't know." Corn said picking his head up.

"You think this is my fault?" I asked looking over at Corn.

"It's nobody's fault. There's no excuse for what Rae did. She made a bad decision and now she's gone. I guess she was hurting far worse than anybody thought. Maybe she didn't know any other way out. Babe, I don't know what was going through her head. You knew her far better than I did."

"I just hate it had to end this way."

I sat there for hours just thinking about what Rae did and trying to figure out why she did it. I just couldn't make sense of it. I understand wanting somebody to hurt but I don't understand wanting somebody to die. I can't help but wonder why she didn't murder me too. I guess love can make you do some strange things and sometimes love can kill you. I'll never get over the part I played in this tragic story.

I laid my head down on my fluffy couch cushion and suddenly there was a knock at the door.

"Who is it?" I yelled.

"It's Kyle." A deep voice answered.

I looked over at Corn. "Do you know a Kyle?"

"No, I don't think so." Corn said getting up off the sofa and opening the door.

There was a tall, light skinned handsome man standing in the doorway. He looked so familiar to me. I knew I had seen this man before.

"Hi Sasha. It's me, Kyle Johnson." The handsome man said.

"Daddy?" I whispered out loud.

"Yes. It's been a long time. Can I come in?" He asked.

"Of course you can, Man. I'm Cornelius, Sasha's husband." Corn said reaching for his hand and ushering him into the house.

"Please have a seat." Corn said. I looked at him upside his head like he was crazy.

"Sash, I know it's been a long time…"

"Yeah, twenty years!" I snapped.

"Baby, don't be like that. Listen to what he has to say. He is *still* your father." Corn said squeezing my hand.

"I'm sorry I just left the way that I did. I think about you all the time. I watched you grow up from the sidelines but I was always so afraid to show my face. I was afraid that you hated me." Kyle said coming and sitting closer to me.

"What do you mean, *you watched me from the sidelines*?"

"Well, who do you think sent you the money for college? I'm also the one that wrote that three hundred thousand dollar check when your grandmother died. I have pictures of you all over my desk. I love you so much. You're my one and only."

"If you loved me so much, why didn't you come back? Why did you throw me out on the freeway and allow me to be hit by two cars? You knew I was living in that rat hole with Aunt Lyla; why didn't you let me stay with you? I hated staying in the projects! Why didn't you come and save me? How come you never even called to apologize for all the hell you put me through? How come when Mom died, you didn't even bother to come to the funeral? I needed you!" I yelled at him.

"I'm truly sorry for throwing you out into the street. I let my anger get the best of me. I hated myself for a lot of years for that day. I can only pray that you'll forgive me someday and begin to love me again. And as far as that other stuff you mentioned, I didn't know until it was time for you to graduate high school that you were living in the projects. I sent Lyla five thousand dollars a month for you so that you two could move into a house in a better area. Lyla told me that you guys had moved to the west side in the better homes. She lied to me. And she lied to you too. She didn't have breast cancer; she was a crack head and a heroin addict. She smoked and sniffed up all the money that I sent you every month. I didn't find out about your mother until it was already too late. Sasha, I'm sorry."

I almost couldn't believe what he was saying but I knew it was true because it made so much sense. I don't remember Aunt Lyla bringing home not one bottle of medicine or papers from the doctor or anything. I don't remember her ever mentioning her doctor's name either. I can't believe my aunt played me like that. She knew how I was working like a dog and skipping school to pay her bills. How could she do that to me? I thought she cared about me!

"Do you hate me, Sash?" Kyle asked with a sincere look.

"Why were you so mean to Mom? Why did you beat her? All she ever did was love you. Why? As far as I'm concerned, you killed her. It's your fault she committed suicide." I said crying out dry tears since I had no tears left.

Kyle looked down at his feet. "I...I don't know. I was using steroids to make me bigger and learned first hand how dangerous the side effects were. Those needles turned me into a monster. That's not an excuse but that's why I was so vicious at times. I'm so sorry. You're right. I did ruin both you and Dyann's life. I take full responsibility for that. I hope you don't hate me. That's why I finally swallowed my fear and decided to come and see you. Sasha, I would like a second chance. Please give me the opportunity to make it up to you. I can make this right. Please allow me back into your life so we can be a family again." He said wiping away a tear with the back of his hand.

"I'm a different person now. I'm not the man that I used to be." He continued.

Right at that very moment, those familiar words sent chills through my body. God wanted me to forgive this man. I had to forgive this man the way that God forgave me; the way that Corn forgave me. Matthew 6:15 says, "For if you don't forgive men when they sin against you, your Heavenly Father will also not forgive you." I learned that scripture in Sunday school last Sunday. What an appropriate time to remember it. I guess this was an easy tradeoff. God won't forgive me if I don't forgive my Dad and turn away from the past. Pastor Harvey always says you can't move forward if you're too busy looking backwards.

I looked up at him. "You know what? For a long time, I hated you more than anybody else in this world. I wanted you to die. But now that I'm an adult and know that people aren't perfect I feel a little differently about you. Um..." I struggled looking for what I was trying to say.

"I forgive you...and I don't hate you." I struggled to say.

He stood up and gave me a tight firm hug. "I really want to be in your life, Sasha. I'm so sorry you had to go through so much as a child. Please give me the opportunity to make it up to you. You are my only child and I love you so much." He said.

I bent down and picked CJ up out of his baby seat. "Meet your grandson, Cornelius Junior. We call him CJ for short." I said handing him over to Kyle. He held him out in front of his chest and began to cry.

"This is the most beautiful baby boy I've ever seen. He looks just like you, Sash! My grandson! Oh, I love him already." He said pulling him closer and laying CJ's head on his chest.

As I watched the baby fall asleep on Kyle's chest, so much joy had begun to jump in my spirit. I didn't know why I was so happy to see CJ and Kyle together. I guess maybe I felt like Kyle wasn't exactly there to watch me grow up but at least he'll be there for CJ. I think this is a start of a beautiful relationship. I can't wait to call Kyle "Daddy" again.

Who am I kidding?

Chapter Seventeen

"His praises shall continually be in my mouth!"

       "Corn, we are going to be late for church! What are you doing?" I screamed from the front door while tapping my foot on the tile walkway.

"I'm coming, I'm coming! I just had to call Kyle to make sure that he was ready to go. You think we should make some extra bottles or snacks for the baby?" Corn said power walking toward the front door.

"No, I packed some in his bag. Daddy will make some extra bottles if he needs to. Are we meeting them at church or what?" I asked pulling Corn out the door, shutting the door behind him and running to the car.

"Yeah, they're meeting us at church."

       I sat back in my seat inhaling the new car smell coming from the leather seats of my new 2006 Lexus GS that my daddy bought me for my birthday this year. I guess he's trying to make up for all the years he wasn't there. He's spoiling me and CJ rotten. He's already put twenty thousand dollars in a college fund, he's bought me this car, and he's bought CJ probably enough clothes, diapers and milk to last a life time. I don't know what could have happened in a short seven months but whatever it was I'm sure happy it happened. I love my daddy so much. He is the sweetest most generous man in this world.

We finally arrived at the House of Praise Fellowship Church thirty minutes later. We pulled up at the same time Daddy did. He looked so nice in his black and white Armani pinstripe suit, his crisp freshly ironed white shirt and his black Gucci dress shoes. I must admit, my daddy has it going on. He has more floozies after him than Pastor Harvey does. Daddy picked the baby up out the car and met us at the front door. He gave me a kiss on the forehead and gave Corn a one armed hug. We went in and the praise began. I never miss the opportunity to praise God. You never know when it may be your last time. I praise Him like I'm losing my mind each and every Sunday. I'm not one of those people who need a pastor to pump me up. I come with an intentional praise! I normally dance all the way to my seat and pass out once I get there. Some people just don't understand how good God is. I don't understand folks that come to church, sit on the back row and be reserved. Was Jesus reserved and dignified when he fought to save a dying world? Was he dignified when he died on the cross for our sins? I think not.

It was now time for the sermon, *my favorite part of service.* Today he talked to us about making God a priority and what you have to do in order for the Lord to take you higher. He told us that you have to go through some *thangs* in order to be ready to go to the next level. Sometimes being a follower of Christ ain't all peaches and cream. It's not always sweet. Sometimes it's very bitter but in the end you'll receive such a joy that all the hell you went through here on earth will soon be forgotten. I can't wait for that day.

God allowed me to go through some things because he had a plan for my life. He had something that He wanted me to do and He needed me to be ready. I accepted my calling to the ministry five months ago. I've become very active in the church and in the community. I share my story with as many people that I can. I speak at different seminars all across the nation. Pastor Harvey, myself, Corn, and many others have formed this evangelistic group called The Power House. We have a television show, a radio show and we do several conferences and workshops each year.

"That was an awesome sermon at church today!" Sister Vanessa said holding the exit door open for me.

"Yeah, God really blessed me today." I replied running out the door.

Sister Vanessa is one of those church members who pretend to be sincere but really she's trying to get up in your business and in the process tell you a little bit of someone else's. We go through this every Sunday.

"Girl, did you hear about Nina and Brother Peterson having an affair? I heard they've been sleeping together for like five years or something crazy like that." She said in a soft sneaky voice.

"I really don't care about that. You need to stop worrying so much about other folks and make sure that *your* life is in order." I responded shooing her away with my bible and walking away. She got the point and went on to the next person with those stupid church rumors. *Lord knows I was in no position to pass judgment.*

I met Corn, CJ and my father at my dad's Hummer. He always takes us to Golden Corral after church on Sundays. That has become my favorite restaurant. They have the best mashed potatoes.

On our way to the restaurant, all I could think about was how far my dad and I have come. I knew it had to be God. That's the only way this relationship could have ever worked. I watched him and Corn sitting in the front seat laughing and talking about sports. I would have never guessed that I would ever see something like this. Then I think about everything that Corn and I have gone through together. I thank God for CJ because I truly believe that had I not had CJ Corn would have left me for good. I thank the Lord everyday that the DNA test proved once and for all that Corn is the father of my child. The day I found out, I was turning cartwheels. Corn doesn't treat me any differently than he had before and he's a wonderful father. In fact, everything that happened has actually indirectly made us stronger.

I still miss Rae dearly and I think about her just about everyday. I think about what would have happened if Sylus and I had never slept together or gotten involved in any way. I sometimes wonder how different my life would be. If I don't know anything else, I know that God has a plan for my life. I think we determine when our destinies will be fulfilled. I avoided God for many years before I finally accepted my calling. But by His grace, God always has a plan B, and plan C, a plan D and so on. God actively pursued me. God will have His way. God gave me a million chances and I'm so thankful that he chose me. I'm so blessed that he found me worthy enough to use for His greater good.

I must admit I miss Sylus too. I miss him so much. I think about him from time to time. As angry and disgusted with him that I became, I still truly loved him and I even love him to this day. It was very hard for me to cope with his untimely death. The same day that I found out that he was killed, I received a letter in the mail from him. The letter was so sincere and it made me feel as though he was still with me sitting right in the same room with me with his arms wrapped around me.

Sasha,

I know it has been a while since we've spoken but I didn't want to keep going on with life as if nothing ever happened between us. I also didn't want you to think that my silence meant that I didn't care about you because I do. I haven't been able to keep you off my mind since our sins erupted and blew up in our faces. I want you to know that I never stopped loving you. I've never experienced a love like ours. What we had was wrong and cold but at the same time it was beautiful and it ignited something in me that I didn't even know existed. I miss you so much even though I shouldn't. I miss the smell of your perfume and the smell of your shampoo. I miss the way your lips and your body felt against mine. When we were together, I felt like we were the only two left on earth and the world was ours. I love you so much, Sasha. It hurts me to my core not being able to be with you. Sometimes I feel like death is better than being without you. I wish I could have you in my arms just one more time. I really don't know what's going to happen between Rae and me but I do know that I'll never love her the way that I love you and she'll never love me the way that you did. There's no love that she could give me that could stand to yours, which is why I'm ending my marriage to her. My love for her is artificial. I don't think I ever truly loved her. I want to give her the chance to experience what love really feels like. I want her to feel what I feel for you. I want her to be happy. She won't ever feel that with me because my heart, my soul and my love belongs to you. I hope I'll see you again someday. I'm looking forward to it. I love you.

Yours truly,

Sylus

I never shared that letter with Corn nor do I plan to. I pray that Rae and Sy are resting in peace. "I love you guys," I said looking up at the sky and blowing a kiss to them hoping that their spirits catch it.

I watched the trees blow and the grass tremble in the wind. I remember once wishing that God would turn me into ashes and let me blow in the wind so that I could finally be free. But he's done something much better than that. God has not only freed me from my agony and pain, he has also freed my mind, my soul and most importantly he has freed me with the power of forgiveness. I'm finally out of bondage and His praises shall continually be in my mouth.

Stand fast therefore in the liberty wherewith Christ has made us free and be not entangled again with the yoke of bondage.

Galatians 5:1

Part II coming soon...

Burned!

If you are an undiscovered author and would like to be published, please send me an email at VictoryByDesignPress@Yahoo.com. Give me your name, title and genre of your work, and what the book is about.

God Bless You

www.ingramcontent.com/pod-product-compliance
Lightning Source LLC
Chambersburg PA
CBHW052148170626
46812CB00004B/1641